JULIA'S HOUSE

BOOKS BY MARIA GRIPE
(*available in English translation*)

PAPPA PELLERIN'S DAUGHTER

JOSEPHINE

HUGO AND JOSEPHINE

HUGO

(*a trilogy*)

THE NIGHT DADDY

THE GLASSBLOWER'S CHILDREN

THE LAND BEYOND

JULIA'S HOUSE

Julia's House

by *MARIA GRIPE*

WITH DRAWINGS BY
Harald Gripe

Translated from the Swedish by
Gerry Bothmer

A Merloyd Lawrence Book

DELACORTE PRESS/SEYMOUR LAWRENCE

Originally published in Swedish
under the title JULIAS HUS OCH NATTPAPPAN
by Albert Bonniers Förlag, Stockholm
Copyright © 1971 by Maria Gripe
English translation copyright © 1975
by Dell Publishing Co., Inc.
Manufactured in the United States of America
First printing

Designed by Ann Spinelli

Library of Congress Cataloging in Publication Data

Gripe, Maria, 1923–
Julia's house

Translation of Julias hus och nattpappan.
"A Merloyd Lawrence book."
SUMMARY: When rumor has it that Julia's house is
going to be torn down, she and her "night daddy" Peter
try to find a way to save it.
I. Gripe, Harald, 1921– ill. II. Title.

PZ7.G8875Ju3   [Fic]   74–22632
ISBN: 0-440-04413-8
ISBN: 0-440-04476-6 lib. bdg.

JULIA'S HOUSE

PETER

WHEN JULIA AND I wrote our first book, I found it very hard to get started.

"You have to start from the beginning, of course," said Julia.

That wasn't much help. But then she added that you probably never know where things begin and where they end.

"So we had better start right away," she said.

She began our first book, and this time it's my turn. That's only fair, especially since she, for some reason, doesn't feel like doing it. I'm not even sure that she'll write a line of this book, and besides, she claims she can't write. I find that

strange because the last time she was so enthusi-
astic!

But maybe she's only pretending so that I'll
plead with her. After all, you can pretend without
being aware that you're doing it. I've done it
many times. Sometimes when people call and
want me to come and talk about stones, I give
them a flat no. If they don't insist I'm relieved.
But afterwards there's an empty feeling inside, as
if I were losing out somehow.

On the other hand, if they do insist and make
me say yes, I of course grumble and sigh, but
when I find myself standing there and talking
about stones again, everything seems right somehow. Then I realize that I was only pretending
when I said no. In some mystical way the stones
seem to take on more meaning if I'm persuaded
to talk about them, because then I know I'm not
the only one who cares. Sometimes I need that
reassurance.

Maybe Julia is having the same kind of feelings
—she needs to be convinced how important it is
before she starts to write. I agree. You have to be
sure before you start. The last time it was different. That book came about because Julia had to
prove to her classmates that I was real.

They seemed to think that I was a great big lie.

2

A night daddy couldn't be a real daddy, they said, and so Julia felt that we had to prove that people like us also exist, not only the ordinary families with mother, father, and children. She felt the book might make them understand a bit, so that they would treat her better and not make nasty remarks. That's how she felt at the time. But I'm not so sure that things have changed much for her. . . .

Of course they came to realize that I wasn't a big lie; it's just too bad they didn't accept me as a person before I got into the newspapers. Then some of the parents began to say to their children:

"Look at this! Today's paper has an article about Julia's night daddy!" And the children could tell by their parents' voices that it was something special to get your picture in the paper. Many people seem to think so. You're in the company of actors, politicians and celebrities —at least that's what they imagine.

So of course Julia's classmates looked at my picture in the paper, and when they saw Julia in school they thought she was looking very smug. But poor Julia had no idea that my picture was in the paper.

"Stuck-up!" they yelled. "You think you're quite something, don't you?"

Soon everyone was saying that Julia was giving herself airs about me, and she still didn't have a clue about why they were annoyed. What had she done wrong?

"Stop pretending!" they said. "Of course you know."

They were going to put her down so that she wouldn't be "stuck-up" again, and they did a good job. In that way they are very clever.

But they didn't mention any of this at home. Their parents might scold them if they made trouble for Julia, who has a night daddy who sometimes appears in the newspapers.

And Julia doesn't talk to her mother about it either. It hurts to have to admit that once again she has managed to have everyone against her. She feels that there must be something wrong with her, somehow.

So who's to say if life has become any easier for her?

That's why we have things to discuss. And there are many things that are easier to write about than talk about. She has said so herself.

Those rumors, for instance—if they're true—what's going to happen around here?

It doesn't seem possible that they're planning to tear down this beautiful old house. And wreck this lovely garden? It's hard to believe that any-one could be that short-sighted. It's just about the only attractive property left in this part of town. But of course crazy things happen when money is part of the game, and naturally, the property will increase in value if they put up an apartment building which will house more people. The land is owned by the city, and if that is what they're planning to do, why don't they first talk to the people who live in the house? If she knew about it, Julia's mother would have said something, so it's obvious that they haven't said anything to her.

Julia doesn't seem to have heard the rumors either. Usually children get wind of every-thing. . . . Anyway, no smoke without fire—I have to find out what's going on. Those people who were charging around here last week couldn't have made it up.

Then one day I became really furious. A man and woman marched right into the garden and started wrecking the chestnut trees, breaking off huge branches to take home and put in vases. They probably hadn't expected anyone to be around, and looked rather embarrassed when they caught sight of me.

"When the house is torn down the garden will go too," said the man.

5

"I haven't heard anything about that," I said.
Then they became downright rude.

"Maybe that's because it's none of your business," said the woman, trying to act superior. And they continued breaking off branches with great snapping and crackling sounds.

Then I chased them away. It's hardly ever possible to reason with vandals. At first they took their time about leaving, but when Smuggler came soaring through the air and brushed past their heads they took off like scared trolls. When he bores those big eyes straight through people he can look terrifying.

Now that he's free he has become much livelier. He obviously enjoys living his own life. It's much better for him and he hasn't dropped us. He comes to visit almost every day, either to my place, or to Julia's. His wings and feathers have become strong and beautiful from all the outdoor exercise, so now he is handsomer than ever.

The only problem at the moment is that he has begun to contribute to the household. When he comes home he usually brings goodies along. Of course that's very nice of him, but it's obvious that our tastes do differ. However, I can't let on. I can't hurt his feelings.

For instance, right now, there is a fieldmouse steak on the table in front of me. I've tried to make Smuggler understand that I'm full and want to save it until later. This time he agreed. But he doesn't always. Sometimes he gets it into his head that he wants to feed me. That's a bit tricky. If he doesn't get me to open my mouth, he tries to stuff the delicacies in my ears. The only way I can avoid that is by using earmuffs. Then he usually lets me save it until "later" if I show him that I appreciate his generosity. And I really do. Enormously. This generosity is also an indication that he's happy now. Before we let him go, he only thought about himself. He was the world's greatest egoist. Now he isn't at all like that.

Just now he is sitting quietly on my head. He knows since way back that I write and think more clearly when he is perched there. He's just about the right weight for my thoughts. This way they stay together and don't whirl around so much, and that's what I need.

I haven't said a word to Julia about the house being torn down. There is no point in upsetting her. But I want to write about it now because I have a strange feeling that something is about to happen. And so, by the time Julia reads this—if it

should develop into a book—we'll know what has
happened to the house. Should the worst happen
—of course we can't let it, but *if*—it might be
useful to have some kind of record right from the
very beginning. Afterwards you never remember
details—at least I don't. Julia's memory is much
better.

We're going to do this the same way we did it
the last time—neither one can read what the
other has written until the whole book is finished.
Julia isn't even going to read her own, she says,
and besides there might not be anything to read.
But who knows?

There is a chestnut tree outside the window. You can almost see the buds growing, which means that summer will soon be here.

What's going to happen? Naturally I can't help wondering. . . .

JULIA

O.K. I'll give it a try.

Can you imagine what I heard in the dairy yesterday? One lady said to another lady that I was much too big to need a night daddy. Can you believe it! But that's probably the way people think. You never outgrow ordinary, or as it's called, "natural," mothers and fathers. You're allowed to keep them all your life because they're "obligatory," or whatever it's called when you're not allowed to choose, yourself. But other kinds—night daddies, for example—supposedly you get too old for them. What kind of sense does that make?

I'm sure people write books about things less important than this, and that's why I'm sitting here again with my ball-point pen, although I'm not at all sure that I want to.

The last time we wrote, it was my idea. I was the one who wanted to do it and kept on pestering Peter because the book was supposed to be about him and me and I was thinking about us all the time. It was as if we were the only two people in the world—and Smuggler too, of course.

But that was when I was very young. Those were the times when my head could hold only one thought at a time and I was able to think it through to the end. Then I always knew exactly what I wanted to write, and I thought that Peter was terribly lazy because he could never get started. But now I understand.

(Peter is my night daddy. The last time I didn't want to give his name—I wanted to keep it a secret. I hardly wanted to say it myself—at least not out loud. I thought that it might make him disappear, although sometimes I would whisper "Peter" very, very softly. What a baby I was then!)

I don't want to write the same kind of things— about Peter and everything we said to each other —our thoughts and things like that. I really don't want to write another book about us. It was different when I felt so insecure. And books do take such a long time to read. . . .

This time it's Peter who wants us to write.

But I can't keep my head together the way I did when I was younger. New thoughts keep on coming into it—masses of them at the same time. And my feelings change from one minute to the next. It's a very odd sensation.

Sometimes I suddenly remember something I did or said or thought a week or so ago, and then it strikes me that I would never do or say or even think such a thought today. I'm always changing my mind and it's so exhausting! I've probably always done it but I do it much faster now. Before, it used to take me a month to change my mind.

The things I remember weren't terrible, no lies or things I was ashamed of or anything like that. They are just ordinary things which I hardly gave a second thought to when they happened; that's how unimportant they were at the time, although they struck me afterwards. What strikes me particularly is suddenly knowing that you can never repeat them. A funny feeling.

Since I know that my mind changes so quickly, it doesn't quite make sense to write a whole book. I guess the only solution is not to read it. But

Peter really insists on doing this book now, although he knows how I feel about it.

"It will make your head feel better," he says.

"But not yours, when you see what I have clobbered together," I told him.

"Oh yes, it will," he said. "You know how worried I feel when everything gets all jumbled up for you. And vice versa."

That's true. When his head is messed up, I feel terrible. I get all involved before I know it. But these days he is rarely down. He has finally taken those old exams, and now he has some kind of degree, and writes a lot for the newspapers and gives lectures. Naturally, it's about stones. His book about stones will soon be finished. It's going to be very fat. Ours won't be anywhere near that size.

So Peter has had a lot on his mind. But towards me he's been the same as ever, only now we know that he can do a lot of things that grown-ups care so much about. When we first got to know each other he was just my night daddy. Then no grown-ups took him seriously, and they made that quite clear. "Oh, yes, that night daddy with his stones," they would say. But now they talk about the stones as if they were very valuable. Then porphyry and mica were worthless; now they sound like the clinking of gold in their ears. But they are the same stones because stones don't change.

Peter has more money now. Not much more money, but more. Before he was poor as a church-mouse. But he didn't care. He just laughed about it.

"I can afford to be poor," he would say.

That was quite a while ago. But yesterday I remembered that he used to say that. I asked him how he felt about it now, if he could still afford to be poor. He thought about it for a while and then he said:

"Yes, but it isn't free any longer."

What did he mean? He didn't laugh when he said it. Peter often says things that take some time to understand. That's why I don't forget them because I know that some day I'll know what he meant. And I don't need to understand everything all at once. That's why we get along so well.

I wanted to tease him so I said: "Peter, can you afford to become rich?"

"Huh?" he said.

"Can you afford to be rich?"

He glared at me.

"I mean if it were free," I said.

"I don't know," he said, and that puzzled look,

14

which he sometimes has, appeared. He added that to be rich probably wasn't free either.

Although I had only been joking, he looked sad, so to cheer him up I said: "You probably won't get rich on stones." I don't think he'll have to worry about that! Then he laughed and told me to lay off and not bother him with sticky questions. But I don't understand—what was so sticky about them?

Peter, though, is an expert at asking sticky questions—which he forces you to answer. But that's all right because I've noticed that most grown-ups always ask children questions which they've already answered themselves. For example, if they see that you're having a good time they ask you if you're having a good time. It makes you feel so funny. So I only answer when it's obvious that they don't know, and don't have any idea what I'm going to say. Otherwise there's no point. . . .

Some grown-ups also heap praises on everything you do. I don't like it because you never know whether it's to console you because you don't know any better. They think you can't do something and then they flatter you to cheer you up, even if their thoughts are running in the opposite direction.

Peter never does that. He very seldom praises, because he always means what he says (when he isn't joking, of course).

"If you have trouble with your thinking you can borrow Smuggler," he said the other day. "Smuggler usually helps."

When Peter has trouble collecting his thoughts he lets Smuggler sit on his head, because then things seem to settle down inside it. But those are *his* thoughts, not mine. On *my* head, Smuggler does no good at all. How many times do I have to keep on repeating that he isn't big enough? I would need at least an elephant sitting on my head.

"O.K. I'll make one for you," said Peter.

I thought he was joking, but the next day he came with a mass of cloth and feathers and tassels and stones and wire, and all kinds of other things which he had gathered together for me, and which I'm supposed to put on my head when I'm thinking. In one way it looks like an elephant—in another way it doesn't.

"It's a winged creature," said Peter solemnly, "although the wings aren't quite developed yet, because it's only a baby. But it will soon be ready to fly."

I said I thought it was a great idea to put wings

on elephants, which are so heavy and could really use wings or something to lift them. How come God didn't think of that? I don't think it's right

that only birds should have wings. They're so light anyway.

"This is an eledront," said Peter, "a cross between an elephant and a dront. Its wings are ideal, as you can see; they don't flap as much as Smuggler's."

The eledront has eyes like stars, mysterious ones. They're blue and sparkling.

He is really very useful. It feels good to have him on my head. He sits still and doesn't move around and make a lot of sounds and flap his wings the way Smuggler does. But if I shake my head a little, he sways up there, in perfect balance, and his wings ruffle. He is very cleverly put together.

"But so is Smuggler," said Peter.

"Smuggler doesn't have star eyes," I said.

"No, but he has moon eyes," said Peter.

He was trying to make him feel better because Smuggler had begun to make his chop-chop noises and was behaving strangely. He makes two sounds: the ordinary hooting when he feels fine and is in a good mood, and the chop-chop sound when he's depressed and feels rotten. Or perhaps afraid. That day he chop-chopped without a let-up. He seemed to be in the foulest mood; he refused to eat, and wouldn't go out.

It wasn't like him. He had been out every day since we gave him his freedom. That was a long time ago. Smuggler was tame from the beginning. But we wanted him to live his own life, which is what we all want to do, so we let him go. At first he disappeared. Then we were a bit upset—we thought that he wouldn't come back, and that we would never see him again. But then he came, came of his own free will, and now he flies all over. It's much better this way because now we know that he comes home because he wants to and not because he has to—not because he needs help. He manages beautifully by himself, but he likes us to make a fuss over him. If we happen to have the radio on and don't hear him outside the window, he's hurt. Sometimes we see a fuzzy figure sitting there glaring at us reproachfully. Then we realize that he's been there for a while and is offended that we didn't let him in immediately. His feathers are all ruffled and he is twice as round as usual. He probably thinks he looks threatening. We have to plead with him for a while before he finally consents to fly in. But then everything is O.K. again, because he doesn't harbor grudges—except the day the eledront came to the house.

I thought that he was probably jealous of the

eledront, but Peter didn't agree. If that were the case he wouldn't have tolerated me either, and he has never been grouchy with me.

Peter thought he was afraid, and that was probably it.

If we were owls ourselves and saw something which looked alive but wasn't, which was just as big as ourselves and looked like a bird but wasn't, and didn't look like any other animal we had met up with, of course we would be frightened too.

But gradually he calmed down. He was only upset the first day, before he realized that the eledront wasn't dangerous. Then it dawned on him that it wasn't real, and after that he completely ignored it. Now he doesn't even bother to look at it.

I'm very fond of the eledront. It was very hard for Peter to make it—it took him a whole night. He wanted to be sure that he had the right shape, the right look, and the right expression in his eyes —the last being the most important. And then, of course, he had to be the right weight, not too light.

"He was made especially for your mysterious, flighty thoughts," said Peter.

I understood what he meant, but I can't help it

if Peter's thoughts weigh more than mine; that's not my fault.

"Do you think you'll be able to write now?" Peter asked.

He doesn't know that I've already begun. That's just as well, because if it comes to nothing, I haven't promised anything definite, only that I'd try. I still don't know how it will work, and I'm not sure whether I'll continue.

PETER

Down at the river the boys are building a paddle boat. They have dissected an old bicycle and made a real paddle wheel which is built into the stern. The wheel is turned by the bicycle, which is placed in the middle of the float. All you do is pedal; the wheel rotates in the back and the float moves forward. Effective and practical. I'll be very interested to see it finished. But what about the steering? I wonder if they've solved that problem yet. It's going to be a big float with a cabin and all kinds of equipment. It looks sea-worthy and I'd like to make one for us. But unfortunately, we'll probably be busy with other things. . . .

I must try to find out what's going to happen to the house. Yesterday two men were sitting outside in the sun, taking a rest, and when I came by I heard them discussing it.

"I suppose they'll make a parking lot of it," said one of them.

"No, row houses I've heard. Seven of them. Everything will sure be different around here."

Yes, everything will be different—especially for Julia. She still doesn't seem to know what's going on; neither does her mother. Otherwise it seems to be general knowledge. In the bookstore the other day, the boy who waited on me asked how long Julia and her mother would be allowed to remain in the house. According to him, the decision had been made, and it was only a question of time.

When I got upset, his response was the usual: "Take one day at a time."

That didn't exactly make me feel any better. . . .

These days there is a strange atmosphere around here. Julia's mother seems to feel that it is "unnecessary" for me to keep on coming here because now Julia is big enough to take care of herself when her mother works the night shift at the hospital. That's what "people" are saying, according to her. Of course Julia can take care of herself. She always did. For that I was never needed. Julia has never been afraid of being alone, either at night or during the day. That isn't the reason I come here.

But as Julia says, even if she has gotten bigger, my room certainly hasn't. I still live in the same old "caboose," and my bed is still full of books and stones—which means that I still don't have any place to sleep. And lately I've collected still more stones and books. But I can work quite well there even though the space is tight.

Also I have to think about Smuggler. Since he is free, he is making greater demands. He visits me mostly in the daytime and I want him to enjoy himself and feel at home. Before he would perch anywhere. He would settle on a book, a stone, a pot, or on my head. And he liked to sit on the telephone—that's where he is right now—but only to keep me from talking into it.

Anyway, I noticed that the creature was becoming restless. He flew from one object to the other, but no place seemed to suit him. Then I brought home a branch, and he settled down on that. He was really a funny sight among the twigs. But the branch wasn't sturdy enough. It was constantly landing on the floor, and there he would sit, making his chop-chop noises. Then I thought of a solution!

I went into the woods and found a sturdy tree stump which I dragged home to Smuggler on a wheelbarrow. That suited him, and now he feels at home.

But then we had to get a stump for Julia's house, too. There he has a real tree trunk with big branches to hop around on, since they have lots of room. So now we have taken care of Smuggler. But I'm more crowded than ever. Julia understands my predicament, and her mother too, but she is so afraid of what "people" are going to think. Because "people" don't understand our arrangement they think it's "peculiar." Well, let them think what they please. We can't change our lives because of them. And we want to be together. We need each other.

I told Julia not to pay attention to what people say. They're always talking. Only Julia and I can decide what is "unnecessary." But she is furious! She is going to show them who is unnecessary, she says. Sometimes she has a terrible temper. It took a long time before she simmered down.

One day she suddenly started to avoid me. I

don't know what it's all about, but that's her business, I suppose. Or is it? Maybe she wants me to ask her straight out what's wrong. I can't figure it out. When she was younger I know she wanted me to. But the past few years she has become more secretive, and I can hardly ask her if she wants me to ask! Sometimes I come very close to it though. Although we know each other very well, it's often hard to know how to act. I think that I'm being myself, but then again I'm not so sure.

And I know that Julia feels the same way when she is trying to talk to me about something.

"Sometimes you're a lot of hard work," she says. But I think I'm my usual self and can't understand what she means. Probably I'm not; it's something I can't judge myself. It seems so hopeless—how can I possibly know anything about others if I don't even know myself? I expressed these thoughts to Julia.

"It's a real problem," I said.

"I think it's exciting!" she exclaimed, looking blissful without any reason at all. So she leaves me completely baffled. That's what's so much fun. It's impossible to get bored with Julia.

By now we have known each other a couple of years, and naturally both of us have changed since we last wrote. Then our friendship was new and therefore exciting. Now we know much more about each other and that makes it even more exciting.

I wonder whether she's started work on the book yet. Perhaps that's the reason she's avoiding me. Perhaps she wants to keep it to herself. In that case I won't ask.

The less you ask, the more you get to know, the saying goes. That can be quite trying for someone like me who is always brimming with questions. Anyway I'm not sure if it is really true. Not always.

I've been thinking about the little boy who stands outside the fence looking into the garden every day. Who is he? Where does he live? He's a little fellow, at the most six years old. He doesn't go to school yet, because then he couldn't be roaming around the whole day. He's always hanging around there, rain or shine. In the morning when I go home to my own place he's there, even as early as six o'clock. Same thing when I come at night—there he is, standing practically on the same spot. Sometimes I wonder if he has a home. But he doesn't seem to be in any need.

He's a funny little figure, always bundled up. He doesn't seem to wear his clothes the way other people do, but to *live* in them. He peeks out from them as if from a tent. It's obvious that he feels at home in them, but his cap is always down over his eyebrows in a way which would make anyone look suspicious. But not this boy. Not with those eyes. They must be the roundest eyes I've seen— next to Smuggler's, of course. Like a small animal he watches everything that moves, and with the same look of wonder. He never seems to get upset

or angry no matter what happens around him.
Not even curious. Just a bit surprised, but not
even very much. A pair of eyes looking as eyes
ought to look when you are really using them,
letting them shine through from within.

Sometimes other children play around him,
but not with him. At first I thought that they'd
left him out for some reason—that they wouldn't
let him play. But it doesn't look that way. I've
never seen them argue. He and the rest just don't
seem to have anything to do with each other,
which must be unusual for children who play on
the same street. You would think that at least they
would notice each other, even if they don't play
together. But they don't even seem to see each
other. It's as if they were invisible to each other—
as if they lived in different worlds. No one seems
to be hurt by this arrangement—not that I can
see, in any case. It's a very odd situation.

The little guy scrutinizes everyone who walks
by. He follows them with those eyes peering out
from under the rim of his cap, but he doesn't
greet anyone. In the beginning I made the mistake of saying hello, but I got nowhere. He looked
at me attentively, though not in an unfriendly
way, but made no sign of greeting. He probably

didn't feel that we knew each other well enough. I tried again a couple of times but then I gave up because I didn't want to look foolish.

He probably doesn't greet anyone—animals don't either when you think of it. At least not the kind of polite greetings we have been brought up with. They do it spontaneously, out of joy. Maybe this boy doesn't have that feeling when he meets people. He just seems to look at them in a puzzled kind of way. It is not that he is shy. Only on his guard.

Now when we meet, I don't say a word, but I look back at him the same way he looks at me, in a friendly and interested way. I think that's the way he wants it.

This is just about all I know about this boy. I don't even know his name or where he lives. I wonder if I'll ever know anything more about him?

Maybe it isn't even necessary. Why not be content just knowing that he exists and that he belongs in this street and in his house? I'm happy when I see him. Isn't that enough? It should be.

But it isn't. Not for me. Unlike the little boy, I'm very curious, and I would be terribly disappointed if he stayed away for a day. I want to know more about him. . . .

JULIA

I FELT IN MY BONES that something terrible was about to happen. It was in the air.

The whole day there was the kind of hazy weather I detest. The sun comes through dully and indifferently. It might as well not have bothered.

It makes no real shadows beneath the trees, but only a blur. Gray spots. It's sad and depressing when the shadows fade away, as if they had no strength. Then I much prefer a gray sky so that you don't see them at all. I like shadows—strong shadows—even my own. Usually, that is. But these days there isn't much life in mine. It looks

like a fish out of water. It makes me tired just to
look at it, and we drag ourselves home from
school, my shadow and I, both of us really down.

So I knew ahead of time that something was
going to happen—nothing would surprise me.
When I got home my whole body felt heavy, and
I could hardly open my eyes. I went inside right
away, although the crocuses were just beginning
to bloom. I just didn't feel like staying out.

I got myself a glass of milk and just sat around.
Peter doesn't get here until six. Mama had already left. She always has a lot of errands to do
before she goes to the hospital.

Then I heard a lot of knocking and banging
and scraping in the walls. It didn't scare me, but I
wondered what it could be. Rats don't sound like
that. It must be bigger animals. And it didn't
sound as if the sounds came from inside.

I went over to the window and looked out, but
I didn't see anybody. Then I heard voices. Men's
voices. So of course I went out, and there were
two men knocking on the wall with an iron pipe,
or whatever it was. They pretended not to see
me.

"Why don't you knock on the door instead?" I
asked.

They didn't answer but just looked stupid.

"My mother isn't at home," I added.

"We're not here to see your mother," said one of the men gruffly.

"If you don't want anything, why are you here?"

They didn't answer but began walking around the house. I trailed behind them. They ignored me, but seemed annoyed. Their car was outside the gate, and one of them went to the car, which was standing there, and fetched a roll of paper. They unrolled it—it was some kind of map. Then they kept pointing to it and whispering so that I wouldn't hear them.

"People who whisper are liars," I said, because by now I was furious. When they didn't answer I repeated it in a louder voice.

"You've got a fresh mouth too," said one of the old men.

"Get out of here!" said the other one. "We've got work to do."

But I didn't budge. I live here, and I told them so, but they just kept on staring at the map, and didn't say any more. There was no point in opening my mouth, so I just hung around. They kept on walking around the garden, dragging their legs and their wilted old shadows. The sun was still no more than a pilot light, giving off its pale glow. I trailed behind them; my head ached and I felt terrible.

Finally they went over to the car. They opened

the door and stood gaping at the house. Then the ruder of the two said:

"This is all ready for demonition." Demonition? What kind of a word is that? I heard it distinctly. It sounds pretty weird, but that's what he said. Can people just make up words? We aren't allowed to do that in school.

When Peter comes I must ask him what it means. Ugh! Just that one word made me think about school. . . .

There things aren't going so well for me. The teacher says that it's because I don't listen, that my thoughts are elsewhere. But is it my fault that there are always so many other things to think about?

The teacher says that you have to concentrate, and think only about the things you're dealing with at the moment. But she can't tell me *how* to concentrate, although I've asked her. The only way is probably to operate and take all thoughts out of your head so that they don't interfere with school thoughts. But in that case they'll have to take the whole head. Good riddance! Sometimes it feels like a beehive filled to the brim with buzzing bees, all lazy drones, and no workers. I don't think there is a single worker bee in my head.

And Ulla and the rest of them haven't changed.

They're exactly the same as they've always
been. . . .

Before, when I was doing well in school, they
used to tease me. They called me teacher's pet,
apple polisher, and all sorts of things. You'd think
that they would be pleased now that things are
going badly. But now they make fun of me because I'm the worst in the class. I'm not! I'm bad,
but not the worst.

Of course I can become the worst, if things continue going in this direction—backwards!

Everything seems so strange—there seem to be
a lot of bad vibrations around all the time. They
are always hanging around talking at school, but
they are almost never happy together because
there's always someone having a rotten time and
being left out. I've thought about that because
I've always wanted to have brothers and sisters,
but now I'm not so sure. I've noticed that you can
be alone even if you have masses of them. And
I'm not alone anymore, no more than I want to
be, because with anyone there are times when you
both want to be, and feel, completely alone. Then
it's all the more fun when you meet. Peter thinks
so too.

Mama thinks that I have spring fever because
I'm having a bad time in school. She says you im-

agine a lot of things when you're tired. But I'm not tired! It is she who ought to be tired—she always has so much to do, and she never has a chance to rest.

I'm glad she wasn't home when those men came. It might have upset her; this house isn't ours, after all.

Maybe they only came here because they were curious. People are always interested in this house because it's so old. When we first moved here I didn't think that there was anything so special about it. We've always lived in old houses, although not as old as this one. Mama says that houses are the same as people—they grow old in different ways. Some become mature with the years but others just deteriorate, she says.

This house seems to have become mature, which means that it's distinguished. That may be, but it certainly isn't distinguished to live in. My classmates say that they would never want to live in such an old house. They say that we live here because we can't afford to live in a modern apartment. I don't know whether that's right or not, but I don't want to ask Mama. It isn't important. Anyway, it's the best house in the world. Of course it's a bit large for only Mama and me. But we should count Peter too, and Smuggler. It's ideal for an owl to have a big place to fly around in—especially with the high ceilings. Now that he is used to flying in the open sky he has to have some room to move around in inside, too. Otherwise the difference would be too great.

Peter has built a cage for Smuggler. The old one was too rickety and confining. He wouldn't set foot in it once he got used to his freedom. The new one doesn't look like a birdcage at all. You can't even call it a cage—it's more like a house. Peter made it out of boards so that it looks like a shed—or one of those outhouses they have in the country instead of a toilet—a real old-fashioned privy, but neat and cozy.

Later. But the same day.

Now I've asked Peter what the word means.

"What did you say?" he asked.

I repeated it.

"Where did you get that?"

I told him about the men, the map, the whole thing.

"That doesn't sound so good," Peter said.

"No, it sounds crazy, but what does it mean?"

Then he told me. There is no such word as demonition. The word is *demolition*. It has nothing to do with demons! It's some kind of fancy word they use to make things sound better than they are.

Peter got terribly angry and said it was a scandal, and that isn't all he said. Those men had no right running around our garden talking nonsense, and now he was going to find out what was behind all this. And he would like to ask to see that map of theirs and then tear it into shreds.

Now those men will have to explain what they were doing around here. They won't be able to get away with just being rude and claiming that they have nothing to talk to us about. No one can get as angry as Peter, so now they had better watch out. It will serve them right! They looked so stupid standing there!

I have no idea how Peter is going to find them. I described them as best I could, although I can't remember what kind of tie the nastier one was wearing. Brown with dots I think, although I'm not sure, and besides, they might change clothes. I don't think I'd be able to find them myself. The car was gray, one of those hopeless, depressing colors.

But Peter says it doesn't matter. He'll track down someone who is involved. He thinks there may be lots of men behind this, maybe a whole gang. There usually are when they use such

stupid words, now that we know what demonition
—I mean demolition—means. It may be a useful
word to know.

Peter won't let me come along when he deals
with those men. He wants to do it alone, but
afterwards he's going to tell me everything, and
then we'll decide what to do, and put a stop to
this running around in our garden, in case they
should try to come back. Now we'll have to be on
our guard!

But what are they after . . . if I only knew!

Peter has an idea but he doesn't want to talk
about it. Not yet. As soon as he can prove something he'll tell me. Peter is furious with those
men, and so am I. I'd really like to let them know
how I feel about them!

PETER

I STILL HAVEN'T been able to find out anything about Julia's house. I've made a lot of phone calls but it seems impossible to get any information. No one knows anything. No one wants to say anything. They transfer you from one person to the next—everyone passes the buck.

But it's obvious that something is up. Otherwise they wouldn't have to be so secretive about it. All they would need to say is that the house is being torn down. Period. But instead there is a lot of talk back and forth to the effect that nothing has been decided yet. We have to be patient for a while, they say, by which they mean that you're supposed to sit around and twiddle your thumbs until they decide to give you a straight answer.

Not on your life! If I have to turn heaven and earth upside down I'm going to make them tell what they're planning to do with the house. If it appears that they are planning to tear it down, I've promised myself to put a stop to it, and I intend to keep that promise.

Julia doesn't know anything yet, but she is beginning to suspect that something is wrong. Those men who were banging around the other day, and saying that the house was ready for demolition, started her mind working. I've explained the situation as best I could, but I haven't had the courage to tell her straight out that the house is coming down. I want to be sure before I say anything.

I can't get a decent answer from anyone, and I'm so mad I'm ready to explode.

But I can see their minds at work. They think that they can come one day and announce: "Tomorrow you have to move!" First they'll probably have to find us another place to live in, but they seem to have the idea that they can push people around without consulting them just to suit their convenience.

They'll find out!

Elvis Karlsson—that seems to be the name of the funny little kid who is always standing looking into our garden. Julia thinks so too, but she's not sure. She insists that he threw snowballs at her this winter. *That* I find hard to believe. He doesn't seem quite that bold. But Julia says that every day when she walked through the garden, snowballs came flying. They never hit her directly, but they whizzed by her ears. She says he must have been the one, because there was no one else around. He was very clever, though; she never caught him throwing one. No matter how quickly she turned around, he always managed to assume his usual innocent expression.

It's a mystery; the kid doesn't look as if he were particularly quick on the trigger.

"Didn't you throw one back?" I asked Julia.

No, she didn't. He was too little.

"Maybe he wanted to play with you?" I said.

Julia didn't think so. She doesn't see anything strange about Elvis Karlsson. I'm the one who is childish, she says, because I don't get the point:

The kid wants to be left alone. Yes, of course, I understand. I just can't help wondering why he threw snowballs at Julia.

"You show too much interest in him," Julia remarked. "He doesn't like that."

"What makes you think he doesn't?"

"I *understand* him." She sounded as if she didn't understand at all, but I could hear that she didn't want to be contradicted. I felt that I was being stupid, but for some reason I didn't want to drop the subject.

"Then why is he always standing outside the house?"

"He doesn't."

"He most certainly does!"

"You only think he does!"

"I have eyes."

"It doesn't seem that way."

What was this all about? This was most unusual behavior for her. Most of the time we could discuss things. Here we were sitting glaring at each other, and I felt myself getting angry. Julia was already, and all because of that kid! It just didn't make sense. If he had at least done something that was worth squabbling about, but he never does anything—he just stands there!

"He does not!" Julia repeated furiously.

"Yes, but every day when I pass . . ." I began,
but she interrupted me.

She accused me of being illogical. Just because

he happened to be standing there when I walked by didn't necessarily mean that he was always standing there. One could just as well say that he was always standing outside school, or up at the football field, or outside the shopping mall, because he was hanging around there just as often.

"Don't you understand, he gets around," Julia said.

"Does he?" I felt my jaw drop in amazement, and Julia looked foxy, not angry any longer.

"Yes, he does."

"The same boy?"

Julia burst into laughter. It's just awful how stupid you can sound sometimes when you're not thinking. But it hadn't occurred to me that the same little boy, of whom I had become fond from seeing outside this house, also appeared in other places. Of course it was idiotic, but it didn't fit my image of him.

"What did I tell you?" said Julia. "You shouldn't fantasize so much about people."

"You should talk!" I said. No one fantasizes more than Julia.

"This time it was you," she said quietly.

She was right. We didn't talk about it anymore.

I went over to the window to look for Elvis Karlsson and thought that I saw a glimpse of him behind the hedge. Julia claimed that I was wrong. "He isn't there now," she said.

"I would never have thought that he got around so quickly. He looked very stationary to me."

"Does that mean that he stands still while others walk by?" Julia asked.

"Exactly."

"Like a station?"

"Yes."

"Oh."

It was impossible to read her thoughts, and what she put into her "Oh," I never did find out.

I again looked out of the window and could swear that I saw the boy's cap for an instant, as usual pulled way down over his eyes. Then it disappeared. I didn't say anything to Julia.

One thing is certain: Elvis Karlsson hasn't become less interesting because he moves around.

I must admit that at first I was a bit disappointed. I guess I had begun to think that he belonged here. I think I wrote before about my feeling that the little fellow had some connection with us here, with the house and the whole place, as if he were some sort of sprite, or mascot, or belonged there. But that was wrong of me. Perhaps that's the reason Julia reacted so sharply. She probably thought I was trying to acquire Elvis Karlsson in some way and study him. But that's not what I meant. I'm just curious about the boy. Actually he's outside this house more often than Julia will let on. That I know, but I won't talk about it anymore since it seems to be a touchy subject.

Strange how things can get snarled up at times, even when you mean well.

Julia has a man teacher in school—a new experience for her. She has always had women teachers before, but now she has the man teacher for a couple of subjects. He arrived the other day.

Sometimes she talks about him, but it's mainly what her classmates think of him that I get to hear.

"Birgitta's mother thinks he is too young to be a teacher," said Julia.

"And what does Birgitta think?"

"She doesn't think anything."

"And you?"

"Don't know. . . ."

Julia frowned and looked puzzled. She took a big bite out of the sandwich she was eating and stared straight ahead. Then she volunteered that he was probably my age, but different. . . .

"In what way?" I asked.

"Don't know. . . ."

She continued to frown and think about it. She ate two more sandwiches and I read the paper while she was thinking. Then she nodded and said, as if to herself, that Ulla and Birgitta and Kerstin and Birgit and Karin and she, they were also about the same age, but different.

"Haven't you noticed that?" she asked.

"Yes, of course. . . ."

"O.K." said Julia, and seemed relieved.

"What do you mean?" I said, not quite following but having an idea what she was driving at.

"There's no point in comparing people," she said. "It's better not to."

I agreed. I realized that she had been comparing me with the teacher, and of course I would have liked to know how it came out, and to whose advantage. But you don't ask such things, so we didn't pursue the subject.

I suggested that we go out for a while and look for tadpoles, but Julia said she had homework. Odd. Homework didn't usually prevent her from doing what she wanted to do.

"Besides, Tryggve has already brought a tadpole to school," she added. "We have a huge jar in the classroom."

"Tryggve?" I said.

49

"Yes, that's his name."

"Who?"

"The new teacher."

"Oh."

"Everyone says he knows an awful lot and is fantastically talented."

I was informed that Tryggve had traveled all over the world and can speak every language. He plays the trumpet and the guitar and the piano and all other instruments, and he has a marvelous voice. He often participates in contests and always wins.

"What kind of contests?" I asked.

"All kinds," said Julia. "And he wears huge glasses, like saucers, although there's nothing wrong with his eyes. . . ."

"Then why does he wear glasses?"

"Because they're good-looking of course," said Julia.

According to her it was nothing out of the ordinary to wear glasses as an ornament even if you didn't need them.

"Since they are so good-looking, maybe I ought to get myself a pair," I said.

She looked at me with an expression as if I had suddenly lost my mind.

"Why should you wear glasses when you don't need them?" she asked.

"But Tryggve does."

"That's different," said Julia.

What was different about it I never did find out. Maybe because he's a teacher? She didn't say, but I got to hear more about his incredible knowledge in various fields.

He is acquainted with all the animals in the whole world. And he can imitate birds. And of course he is a flower specialist and a star specialist and a food specialist. And tightrope walking is easy for him. And he knows a lot of other things, too, which Julia can't remember right now. That can't be easy, since there are so many things to keep track of! Besides, all of this is secondhand from her classmates, and not from Tryggve himself.

I was dumbstruck. Now I can see why she thought it was pointless to compare me with Tryggve. It's better not to.

I felt that I just couldn't bear to hear any more about this genius right now, so I said: "I think I'll go out and look for tadpoles just the same." As I went out into the garden Julia opened the window.

"But Tryggve doesn't know a thing about stones," she said.

"He can't know everything."

"No," she said, "but they say he does."

She jumped out of the window and went down with me to look for tadpoles because it would be fun to have her own, she said.

I looked for Elvis Karlsson on the sly, but he wasn't around. But I didn't look too carefully.

JULIA

So much keeps on happening all the time that it's very hard to know what to write. There are also some things I'd like to tell about but I don't dare, and it's too bad, although it can't be helped.

If I could only be sure that others had been through the same thing and thought the same thoughts, at least once, it would be easier. I wouldn't feel so stupid if there were at least one person who had felt the same way. I'm always hoping, but that isn't enough. One has to dare, too.

A thing good about books is that you don't have to list all the unimportant things that happen, the things which you can't escape in life. In life you have to be part of everything every minute—even every little yawn—and that can be an awful bore sometimes.

When I write I can decide myself what is unnecessary. But sometimes the strangest things happen. I have written down things which I hardly knew anything about, because when they happened I didn't pay any attention to them. Then after I'd put it on paper I realized that what was happening *was* important, although I hadn't grasped it at the time. So now I see how many important things have slipped by that I'll never know about.

It's ages since I've cried. When I'm supposed to cry I never do, at sad movies and things like that, or when our teacher tells us about sad things that happen in the world. Even though she uses a special voice to make us understand how sad it is, I still can't cry, no matter how hard I try. I seem to stiffen inside and don't feel a bit sad. When you notice that she is trying to make you feel that way on purpose, and you feel it's your duty to put on a sad face, it doesn't work. All it does is make me noisy on the outside, while inside I'm stiff and cold as ice.

If she would only tell what happened without that voice, and give suggestions as to what could be done about it, and things like that. Instead, all we do is sit there and feel rotten. We can't say a word because everyone has a bad conscience, and that was her intention because in our country we are so well off. But who is helped by our having a bad conscience and feeling ashamed?

Once when the teacher told sad things about children who didn't get any food and died of sickness or were killed by soldiers, the bell rang.

The door opened and another teacher came in. Our teacher stopped right in the middle of what she was saying and began *laughing*. In the flash of a second she was laughing out loud and talking about something else.

She couldn't have been as sad as she sounded, because how could she have gotten over it so fast? It's only to *teach* us to feel sadness and pity and things like that, that she sounds that way. I don't think you can teach people those things, not that way. It's just like in the movies when you can hear by the music that now you're supposed to feel sad. But then I don't. I get silly at sad films, because when things like that start to happen I start cutting up. Not because I want to, but I can't help it. I just don't want others to decide how I should feel.

That's why I almost never cry, at least not when anyone is looking. But when I was younger I cried for all kinds of reasons—when I hurt myself, when I didn't get my way, and childish things like that.

I think it was mostly out of habit that I cried—not out of need. I understood that afterwards, because before I started to howl I often thought, should I, or shouldn't I?

Usually I was able to decide that matter for myself. I wanted it to pay off, of course, because bawling can be very strenuous. You never know how long you're going to have to keep it up before something happens to console you—that is, if you can hold out that long.

But that was before I began howling for real, and I remember distinctly the day I began.

I was around five years old. Mama and I were going to the dressmaker after my playschool. I was miserable because I had holes in the knees of my tights. Mama didn't know about it. When we got to the dressmaker I would have to take my coat off and it would show, and of course Mama would be angry. I was always getting holes in my tights—I still do. Pants are much better.

Anyway, I wanted to tell her about it before we got there, otherwise it might be embarrassing for the dressmaker. So I walked along sulking and not knowing how to break the news.

Then we met a blind man on a street corner. Suddenly he was standing before us with a thick striped cane which he was tapping on the ground in front of him; it looked like a sad candy stick. He wore black glasses and his face was terribly pale.

That was the first time I met someone who couldn't see. I didn't know anything about blind people. Mama told me that for them the whole world was always black—always. No light and no color ever. She told it to me just the way it was, right there in the middle of the street, in her normal voice. The blind man slowly walked towards the square. All of a sudden I began to cry, and I didn't have a chance to make up my mind whether I should or not. It just came—terrible violent sobs which scared me. They scared Mama too, because she thought I was sick.

"What's the matter? Don't you feel well?" she asked. She was only thinking of me; she had already forgotten about the blind man. Since she didn't sense it, I couldn't tell her that I was crying because it was a terrible shock that there are people who only see darkness. So I lifted up my coat and showed my ragged tights and told her that was why I was crying. Mama seemed to believe me, but I don't remember if she got angry.

After that I stopped bawling—just like that. I didn't decide not to—I just stopped. But sometimes I would think: Today it's a month since I stopped crying, and today it's three months, and today six months. Then I thought no more about it.

But sometimes I'm ashamed because I had to blame my torn tights and couldn't admit that it was because of the blind man that I was crying. Why, I wonder? The tears no longer hurt so deep down when I said it was because of the tights— and I got that off my chest at the same time. That was part of it, because I can be quite sly, although I don't do it on purpose.

That was the time I learned the difference between crying and crying, and once you've learned that, you don't cry very often—not if you can help it.

But today I cried like a baby again. No one saw me, and no one will know about it because I don't really know why I cried. I've been through worse things without crying—many times.

This is what happened: This morning Mama gave me two crowns because she had been away so much lately, so I decided to go to the candy stand and buy some goodies. There were several people ahead of me, so I had to wait. I heard giggling and carrying on behind me, but I didn't see anybody so I didn't give it another thought.

When my turn came there was no one else waiting, so the lady at the stand talked for a while —she is really very nice. Peter had ordered a newspaper, and she asked me to bring it home and tell him that he could pay her later. Then I bought some caramels and she asked whether they were for me. "Or are you going to give some to your night daddy?" she said. She still calls Peter that because she thinks it sounds funny.

Of course I was going to share them. Caramels were Peter's favorite. Then she asked if I didn't want something for Smuggler too. "How about a few pretty jelly mice?" she said.

We talked a bit about how Smuggler would like that kind—she gave me a lot, and I left feeling very happy.

Then I heard steps behind me, and giggling. It was Ulla, Birgit, and Kerstin. They were the ones who had been behind the stand. They had

overheard the conversation, and now they were
mimicking me and acting stupid.

"Yes, caramels are the little nightpa's favorite
—isn't that just too cute. . . ."

"And of course little Smuggler has to have
little chewy mice. . . ."

They kept it up, although I just kept on walking and pretended not to hear them. That made

them angry, so they came up to me and began
pushing me around.

"You think you're something, don't you? And
you think your nightpa is something special too?"

I tried to get away, but there were three of
them, and they are quite strong, too. They
dragged me down to the river, all the way out on
the boat landing, and said they were going to
throw me in because I was so stuck-up.

But they didn't. Instead they ripped the paper
to shreds, and the bag of goodies also broke, so
that everything spilled out on the landing and
was almost crushed by our scuffling. Then they
calmed down and picked everything up, but I
wasn't allowed to have any because I was such a
nitwit. I didn't get a single piece—it was *theirs*,
they said. Then they ran as fast as they could.

As luck would have it I had told Peter that I
was going to buy a treat for us, and now I didn't
know what to say. I didn't feel like going home
because it's embarrassing to come empty-handed
when for once in your life you are treating someone.

I walked around and stewed for a while and
then took the long way home in order to gain
time. I didn't go the usual way but came from the

opposite direction, and that's the reason I came upon the man. Otherwise I never would have found out about the whole thing.

There he was, standing on the other side of the gate with one of those big easels in front of him, the kind artists use. I knew right away that he was painting a picture of our house. That was all right because it's a beautiful house, but it didn't make me happy—instead it gave me such a creepy feeling. He didn't look creepy though—that wasn't it.

But everything was so still; not a soul in sight, only a slight wind which made the leaves on the chestnut trees flutter; a bird was chirping and the shadows were spread about like giants.

The man didn't see me because he was busy painting, so I very quietly went and stood behind him. I was right. He had just started to paint the house.

"What are you painting?" I asked, although I knew.

"I want to paint the house while it's still there," he said.

Everything stopped inside my head. It sometimes does; I don't understand what people are saying although we speak the same language.

"What?" I said.

"I try to paint all houses that are about to be torn down, you see, so that we at least have a picture of them."

My heart seemed to stop. I couldn't utter a sound. He looked at me and his eyes were sad.

"Everything that's beautiful in this town is about to be torn down," he said.

"But not this house."

"Yes, unfortunately," he said.

When I don't have a chance to think, I act like a big baby, and that's exactly what I did now. I grabbed his hand, the one that was holding the pencil.

"I won't let you paint our house," I said, and plunked myself right in front of the painting. He looked surprised, although he didn't move.

"It's beginning to get dark and I was just about to leave," he said.

Then I let go of him and ran away. After a moment I stopped and saw that he had taken the painting down from the easel and was picking up his things. I hung around until he left, and watched him disappear out of sight.

I still didn't want to go home to Peter. I knew that I wouldn't be able to talk to him the way I usually do, because there were a lot of sad lumps in my throat which I would have to get rid of first.

Instead, I walked down to the river and watched the boys who are building a float. But I sat far away so that they wouldn't see me, because I didn't feel like talking.

After I had been sitting there a while, all the lumps in my throat disappeared, but instead I found myself crying. At first I didn't notice it, but then I felt tears dripping from my chin; my whole face was wet. I was furious because it's never happened before that I've cried and didn't know that I was crying. That was too much, but it was good that I was angry, because I stopped crying right away.

PETER

THE OTHER NIGHT Julia said she was going down
to the candy store and would be gone only five
minutes, but she didn't come back.

At first I didn't worry. She is big enough to
take care of herself, and I thought that she had
probably met someone along the way. I wasn't too
concerned, but as one hour after another passed
and it began to get dark without a sign of her, I
became quite alarmed.

It's very hard to know what to do in such a case.
I don't want Julia to think that I'm treating her
like a baby, or think that I don't trust her. If she

is late sometimes, she has a good reason. But she had never stayed away this long before. How could I be sure that nothing had happened to her?

I tried to keep calm as long as I could and tried to reason with myself. Julia is sensible; she won't get into any trouble. So what if she forgets the time for once! Hasn't it happened often to me? I got hold of myself and waited, but I was really worried.

It was almost dark when I saw her coming through the garden. She was walking very slowly, which surprised me, since she always runs the last bit of the way. I opened the window and whistled. She came up and stopped right under it.

"Hi, aren't you coming in?"

"Yes...."

"You were gone a long time...."

For a while she didn't answer.

"Didn't you go to the candy stand?"

"Yes...."

I didn't want to ask any more questions. She was still standing under the window writing in the pebbles with her shoe. I got a lamp and put it on the windowsill so that she could see better. The light from the window made a checkered pattern on the gravel. She didn't say anything but began to jump hopscotch.

"Do you want me to come out and play with you for a while?" I asked.

"If you want to."

I went out and jumped hopscotch among the light squares for a while, but neither of us did very well because by then it was getting quite dark.

"Now we'll go in and have a bit to eat," I said after a while. "Aren't you hungry?"

"Yes," said Julia. Then she seemed to change her mind, and a strange look came over her face. She said she wasn't hungry because she had eaten up all the caramels she had bought, and the jelly mice which Smuggler was supposed to have.

"I couldn't help it," she said.

"What are you saying?" I said, laughing.

Then I noticed she was dead serious. I thought that perhaps she had a bad conscience since she had wanted to treat me, so I said that it didn't matter, and that Smuggler probably wouldn't miss the jelly mice.

"Those things can happen," I added. "Once on my way here I bought a chocolate bar for you which I ate myself, and then I had to buy a new one."

"But I don't have any more money," said Julia, looking crushed.

"We can buy some tomorrow. I'll give you some money."

But she shook her head and said: "I'm tired of caramels . . . I ate too many today . . . but you can buy some for yourself."

"O.K." I said. "I'll do that."

She nodded gravely and we looked at each other without saying anything, probably both wondering what the other was thinking. I realized that something must have happened, but there was no point in pursuing it.

Instead I said that if she had eaten too much candy she would probably need some decent food now, and she didn't object. We went to the kitchen and got a snack together. Julia was subdued and didn't say much, but she had a good appetite. To get her into a better mood, I asked her how Tryggve was. At first she seemed absentminded and not quite with it, but then she reacted. Tryggve is an endless topic of conversation.

"He can skate too," said Julia. "He's a figure skater."

"Oh. . . ."

"He's been skating on television. Ann-Britt has seen him. He was skating with a very pretty girl with a flared skirt."

"Oh. . . ."

"That was last winter. They won."

69

"What about last summer? What did he do
then?" I thought my question sounded stupid,
but I had to say something besides "Oh" the
whole time. I didn't think that Julia would know
what Tryggve had been up to last summer, but
she was well informed. Tryggve seemed to be
watched very closely.

"He was climbing high mountains," she said.
"He's a mountain climber! He has climbed the
world's highest mountain."

"Oh."

"Otherwise he's a deep-sea diver—when he
isn't climbing mountains, that is."

Her eyes had a dreamy look as she said that
there probably wasn't anything he couldn't do,
adding: "But he doesn't know a thing about
stones!"

I cleared my throat and tried to think of something sensible to say, but nothing came. I began
to regret that I had brought up the subject of
Tryggve. It's easy to get too much of him. Strange
that it should be so hard to get a sensible conversation going about someone who knows so much,
and who is obviously so interesting.

Here Julia sits adding up all the things he can
do while I feel my throat getting scratchy. Julia
gives me an expectant look. Or is it a teasing look?

But I still can't find a thing to say. My head has stopped functioning.

Then Julia told me what a fantastic flier Tryggve is. There is a girl in another class who has an uncle who is an aviator, who has told all about him. Everyone seems to be talking about Tryggve. They all seem to be obsessed by him.

"Strange that he became a teacher," I said drily.

Julia gave me an uncomprehending look.

"I mean, since he can do so many other things —it's a waste for such a person . . ."

"You're wrong! It's people who can do things who should become teachers."

I realized I was making a fool of myself, but I couldn't help it, and felt myself getting irritated.

"Possibly," I said, "but there has to be some rhyme or reason to it. What's his field?"

"Everything," said Julia, and was off in the clouds again.

"I mean, what subjects does he teach?"

"You don't pay much attention to what it says on the schedule when you have Tryggve. He doesn't believe in being forced to go by time, subject, schedules and things like that," Julia explained quietly to her square friend.

"Oh," I said. "Does he teach drawing?"

"No, that's our regular teacher," said Julia. "But we wish we had Tryggve because they say he draws magnificently . . . he's also an artist. . . ."

"Yes, I gathered that," I said.

I heard myself sighing. Julia wrinkled her forehead and gave me a sympathetic look.

"Are you tired?" she asked.

"Very," I said. "I always feel weary when I hear how clever others are."

"But he isn't clever when it comes to stones," Julia said.

I had to change the subject and began talking about Elvis Karlsson. Julia is wrong when she insists that he hangs around other places as much as he hangs around here. That just isn't so. By now I've had a chance to observe his comings and goings.

Of course the kid moves around, but most of the time he still spends outside this house. It's obvious that he's especially interested in what happens around here. But in what or whom? Smuggler maybe?

"Don't you know anything about him?" I asked Julia. "I mean about his home life and things like that?"

Julia shook her head. "No, but I do know that

there are other people standing outside this house," she said. "Maybe you haven't noticed them?"

"No. Who, for instance?"

"Typical," said Julia. "You watch Elvis so much that you don't see what's going on around here...."

She told me that today a man was standing outside here painting. He painted all the houses that were about to disappear, he said.

"Why didn't you tell me right away?" I asked.

"I didn't want to think about it," she said. "Besides, it probably isn't true."

She asked me what I knew and I told her that I had also heard rumors, and that I was trying to find out what it was all about.

"If it's true, what are we going to do about it?" Julia wanted to know.

"We have to try to stop it," I answered, far from confident.

"What do you mean?" said Julia.

"I don't know...."

For a while she sat quietly. I sensed that she was sad and worried. I promised myself to do everything I could to save this house.

"Do you think there's any hope?" she asked.

"Of course there is," I heard myself say. "Lots."

Then she looked at me with those eyes which bored right through me.

"You promise?"

I nodded emphatically. We shook hands on it and talked no more about it.

JULIA

IT SUDDENLY OCCURRED to me that there was a
time when Peter and I didn't know each other—
when we didn't even know of each other's exis-
tence. How lonely I must have felt then, and how
insecure!

I'm glad it wasn't then that I found out that
our house may be torn down, because I would
probably have died. I don't think I could have
survived it. But now that Peter has promised to
save this place, I'm not in the least bit worried.

Of course my mother is important too—she's
wonderful, but I depend on her for other things.

If she promises me candy or something before she leaves, I know that I'll get it when she comes home. With Peter, you never know. He easily forgets things like that.

But when I want to talk about serious things, which Mama never seems to be able to get started on, Peter is terrific. Mama makes a joke of everything and ends up by being irritated. She seems to be too shy or embarrassed to get into such discussions. But not Peter. I can ask him about anything —if it's terrible to die, why we have to have wars —anything that pops into my head.

Even though he says he doesn't know for sure, and that you shouldn't believe him because he's only guessing, you can depend on him. He's like a rock. If he says there isn't going to be a war I believe him, although I know he isn't sure.

I think everyone in the whole world ought to have someone whom they can trust in this way. Maybe then people wouldn't make trouble all the time, and fight and tear down other people's houses, and things like that. If everyone had someone to care about and feel for, there probably would never be wars.

But, of course, sometimes you can be very mean to those you love. Why?

I can be horrible. I have a nasty tongue, and

tease and lie. I say things I don't want Peter to believe, although he does. I intend to tell him the truth afterwards, but sometimes I forget. Then I get furious—at myself really—although I take it out on him instead.

It's very complicated.

But Peter can be sly, too. Sometimes he only pretends that he believes everything I say, although he may have been wise to me from the beginning.

"I wanted to give you a chance to talk it out," he says. "I'm very good at not letting on."

But I don't think he's caught on to this Tryggve business. I'm having a lot of fun, because I've noticed that each time I talk about Tryggve he gets a strange look on his face.

Tryggve is our new teacher, and the girls are falling all over him—including me. I think it's stupid, and I don't really want to, but I do it to be "in." When the girls say that Tryggve is "dreamy," I make noises too, although I really don't think so.

He doesn't look like a teacher. The other teachers look as if they had stepped out of the Stone Age compared to him—even though they're perfectly up to date most of the time.

It's impossible to describe Tryggve. His head is

made up of mostly hair, a beard, a mustache, side-burns and bangs—and enormous eyeglasses. On top of it all he wears a big hat with a long scarf wrapped around the crown. That's only the head.

Then he has a body too, consisting of a lot of fringes and pompoms and bits of cloth that flutter around him. They must be draped on something, so I assume there must be a body somewhere, but probably quite small.

But he does have feet, I'm sure of that. You can see them when he leaves school, because he takes his shoes off and walks barefoot. When you com-pare them with the head, they look small and pale and quite ordinary. I was amazed when I saw them because everything else about him is so un-usual.

I haven't described all of Tryggve to Peter yet. It would be too much: he would think that I was putting him on. What Tryggve is really like in-side is hard to tell, but I think he talks too much. Our regular teacher sticks to the subject, asks questions, gives us exams and things like that. Tryggve doesn't. He just talks and talks. He never opens a book. You have no idea what sub-ject you're supposed to be having when you go to his class. He has probably been around a lot, and

I think he knows a lot, although he brags and bluffs quite a lot, too. In the beginning I wasn't aware of it, and if I hadn't had anyone to compare him to, I probably would have gone all out for Tryggve. But I only pretended because I didn't want to be different from the others. Besides, it's fun to tease Peter. A cloud comes over his face when I talk about Tryggve. It's mean of me, but I can't help it. Peter probably feels that he's lazy in comparison to Tryggve, although he really isn't. It's just hard for him to get started, and that applies to me, too.

Of course, one day I'll confess to Peter that I've exaggerated a bit when describing Tryggve, and that he isn't as fantastic as everyone seems to think. You like him because he's different; there just couldn't be anyone else like him. But you don't learn a thing in his class. All he does is talk and brag. One day I think I'll confess everything to Peter so that he doesn't get an inferiority complex and feel depressed on account of Tryggve.

But I was about to tell about something that happened yesterday and how I behaved like a fool.

Peter was coming in a while, so I went out to the garden to wait for him because Mama had just left.

A car stopped in front of the gate—a fancy car, so I thought there must be some mistake. A couple got out of the car. They had a kid along, about my age. They walked through the gate and came up to me. They were very polite so I got the impression that they were nice people.

"Hello there," said the man. "Is your mother in?"

I told him that she wasn't.

"Is someone else at home?" said the woman.

"I'm home," I said, because I thought it was quite rude to ask such a question since I was standing right there.

She didn't get angry, but laughed, and so did her husband. The kid looked snooty, though.

"This is a beautiful place," said the woman, looking around. "Only you and your mother live here?"

I said that Peter lived here sometimes, and Smuggler too, and then the man said that they had known the people who owned our house a long time ago, before I was born.

"We used to come here and visit often," said the woman. "It was beautiful then, and it probably still is," she said as she pulled out a big bag of caramels. As she was about to offer me some, the kid shot forward and stuck his whole fist in the bag ahead of me. He glared at me as if it were my fault that the candy was offered to me first. Laughing, the woman pulled the bag away from him and said that he would have to wait his turn. I was to help myself first, she said, and I thought it served the kid right, because you don't act that way. Then she asked my name.

"Very pretty," she said. "So romantic, so beautiful."

Then she turned to her husband and said it was too bad that my mother wasn't home, because they would have liked to have a look around the house and relive old memories.

"We had a marvelous time in this house," said the man.

"Yes, absolutely marvelous," said the woman. It was an expression she used often.

"But now it isn't possible," said the man.

"No, unfortunately not," said the woman.

They sounded sad and they seemed nice, so I asked why it wouldn't be possible—that seemed strange to me.

"But nobody is home," said the woman.

"Of course," I said. "I'm here."

Then they laughed again.

"Yes, it does sound stupid," said the man. "But you can't let us in—we're total strangers."

"Of course I can," I said, and let them in.

They were delighted, walked around, looked at everything and admired. But the kid was sour the whole time.

"How different everything is! You can see that times have changed," said the woman.

Then she described how it had looked before and pointed out where crystal chandeliers and mirrors and lamps, etc., had hung. It all sounded a bit silly, but I didn't care. She offered caramels and seemed quite nice.

While she was talking, the man walked around staring at all the doorknobs and locks, and things that interested him most.

"He's crazy about everything that's old," remarked the woman, and that was obvious.

But when they got to the second floor and saw the glazed Dutch oven, they both seemed a little cracked. The man rubbed his hands together, and it almost looked as if he was going to eat it up.

"Look at those doors! A real find!" he exclaimed.

They completely forgot that I was there, so I went to my room. And there stood the kid staring at me. He didn't open his mouth for a minute and then he said:

"Is that supposed to be a desk?"

"As you can see," I said.

"Mine isn't like that," he said. "Mine has pigeon-holes and lots of drawers and a bookcase on top. Where is your typewriter?"

"I don't have any," I said.

"I didn't think so," he said. Then he carefully explained that if you have a typewriter you have to have a different kind of desk, or else you have to have a separate typewriter table, because that is what his father had. "But he has a regular desk too, where he keeps his calculator and the telephones..."

He kept on and on. He couldn't talk about anything but their possessions. He was a terrible bore and a snob, but I couldn't help feeling sorry for him because you have to be pretty miserable to act like that.

I went back to the others. But then I overheard something that made me stop in my tracks. I couldn't believe my ears. The man said:

"Just our luck that nobody is home!"

I was about to tell them—for the third time—that I was home, when the woman whispered:

"We can take the doors with us now, can't we? It won't make any difference to them. They're not using the stove now anyway."

The man bent down to remove the doors. I didn't know what to do. Just then Peter appeared.

"Excuse me, but . . ." he began.

He had Smuggler on his shoulder and his eyes looked black. I saw that he was angry, but they had no way of knowing. The woman began her smiling.

"But how marvelous! Do you live here?" she asked.

"But you don't, do you?" said Peter.

"In a way," said the man. "Our best friends lived here once."

"But now they don't anymore," said Peter. He

didn't sound exactly rude, but his voice was sharp.

The man and woman were obviously confused, but the man pulled himself together and tried to sound casual.

"Well," he said, "to make a long story short, we're very much interested in this glazed Dutch oven. . . ."

"Oh," said Peter. "It's interesting. But here is a very interesting door too, especially from the outside. Shall we have a look at it?"

Up until now he hadn't noticed me, but when he did he gave me a wink, which no one saw but me.

The man paid no attention to what Peter said but rattled on:

"We're in the process of building a little weekend place and this glazed stove is just what we are looking for."

"I don't know what we would do if someone else took it," said the woman.

Peter couldn't control himself any longer.

"What do you mean? Are you trying to make off with our stove?"

The man tried to calm him down.

"Take it easy. We only wanted to have the first

bid," he said. "The house is coming down anyway."

I saw that Peter was about to explode, although he tried to control himself.

"It certainly isn't going to be torn down," he said. "And there is nothing for sale here. Now you had better go. This way please."

"But, my dear young man, we only wanted to discuss . . ." said the woman.

But Peter put them out.

"There is nothing to discuss," he said. "Now will you be kind enough to leave us alone."

They were furious. The man turned crimson and the woman said that she had never been so outraged. The kid also tried to act tough.

"It's a good thing that they're tearing down these old hovels," he muttered.

But I didn't get mad at him. He only said it to get on the right side of his father. Peter also sensed it because he ignored the remark; otherwise he would have answered.

They took their time getting down the stairs; they wanted to show that they weren't being pushed by Peter. Then Smuggler decided to do his thing. He probably sensed that we wanted to get rid of those people as quickly as possible. He is very sensitive to such things.

They had gotten about halfway down the stairs. Peter was standing at the top with Smuggler on his shoulder. Suddenly Smuggler made a fantastic nosedive, brushing their heads with his wings. They rushed towards the door with their arms up and their hair flying in all directions. When they couldn't get it open I helped them, so that they could get out into the fresh air, which is what they needed.

PETER

I've finally found out something about Elvis
Karlsson. I suppose that people you see every day
—always alone and never communicating with
other people—stir your imagination in a very special way. I've never even heard the kid's voice—
he's never uttered a sound in my presence—so
I've had no idea what it's like. I've tried to imagine it, and I imagine it as being small and low-
pitched, but quite gravelly—about the way boar
piglets sound. In contrast to their small, spindly
bodies, they make fantastically strong noises.

Elvis Karlsson must sound something like that.

I just can't imagine his voice being shrill and squeaky. Besides, I've noticed that shrill people are seldom quiet.

Anyway, I know a little bit about him now. It began by my tailing him very discreetly—he wasn't aware of it. I hadn't planned to do it—it just happened. One afternoon when I was on my way to the library, I spotted a little kid coming out of a house up ahead. I recognized Elvis Karlsson and quickened my steps. I didn't want to lose sight of him because I wanted to know where he was going—whether it was to our house or somewhere else.

Just as I walked by a certain house—a gray wooden house, very close to where I live, and also where the lady from the candy stand lives—a window opened on the ground floor and a woman stuck her head out and shouted, "Elvis." I gathered it was his mother. Now, I thought, I'll finally have a chance to hear his voice. But no. Elvis didn't even turn around. He just kept on trudging along. The woman called a couple of times and then she banged the window shut. Elvis continued walking down the street, stopping twice to look in a store window. Both times he kept standing there for quite a while. He was probably looking at some special object—at least that was my guess. His first stop was a flower shop. After he left, I also stopped there to try to figure out what he had been looking at so intently. But all I saw were masses of bulbs and seeds. As a centerpiece there was a huge artificial sunflower, probably made of plastic.

The other display window was a toy shop, and there I saw a model, an unusually well constructed sailboat, which I must have been staring at quite a long time myself, because when I looked up Elvis was gone.

I ran to the corner and looked in all directions, but he had vanished. Then I gave up and went to the library.

I've walked by that gray house several times since, and each time I feel as if I had found another piece of the puzzle that is Elvis Karlsson. I'm beginning to get quite a clear picture of what his life is like.

As I said, he lives on the ground floor. His mother spends most of her time talking with people who pass by. There's always someone under that window, often a dog owner.

The mother also has a dog—a little yapping dachshund on whom she seems to lavish all her love. Actually Elvis got the dog as a Christmas present, but the mother was so enchanted with it that now it's hers. Their neighbor, the lady at the paper stand, told me.

So in a way you could say that Elvis lost both his mother and his dog. That happens quite

often, and it's no fun for the one who gets left behind. The mother has told the neighbors that Elvis is giving her a hard time because he's out all day, instead of staying around the house.

But why should he stay home? To listen to his mother gossiping with the neighbors on the street, or on the telephone? Or to watch her play with the dog? Or to listen to the radio, which she leaves on all day? I tried to picture his life.

There is never a quiet moment in that house, but no one has a word to say to Elvis. I can understand why he has become so silent. There can't be much point in trying to make himself heard. There is no one to listen to him. His father reads the paper and watches television when he comes home. Once in a while his mother talks to his father. They talk about money and food, and things that have to be bought or paid for. Sometimes they talk about Elvis and how impossible and hard to handle he is, but they seldom talk to him.

That's why Elvis prefers to get out and be by himself. His parents are strangers to him, and it's better to be with strangers in the street. At least you don't know what they're like. At home he knows them—inside out—that's why he disappears.

Suddenly his mother will appear at the window calling his name so that half the town can hear her. She wants to know where he is, or else she's telling him that it's time to eat. Sometimes he'll dash home, especially if it's a question of food, but just as often he doesn't bother.

Let her stand there and yell. Someone is bound to come by with whom she can gossip. Besides, she has the radio, the dachshund, and the telephone. It probably doesn't bother her if he doesn't show up. She thinks he's very disobedient, that's all. And of course he is. Elvis Karlsson never listens to his mother. That's what the lady at the candy stand says, and everyone agrees—including Elvis.

But his mother never does what Elvis asks—she never listens to him. No one ever mentions that, because no one ever gives it a thought. But while the newsstand lady was talking to me, the same thought kept churning around in my head: Why should only one person have to listen and obey— and always the small one? Why should that be taken for granted? But when I mentioned that to her, she said:

"But of course Elvis Karlsson has to listen to his mother!"

Why couldn't they both listen to each other? Since she is a nice lady she immediately said yes, that hadn't occurred to her. After a moment she added that she did feel a bit sorry for Elvis Karlsson after all, but he was so insolent and so cocksure that she didn't know what to think. . . .

"There's no point in trying to reason with him," she said. "All he does is run away—he wants to be left alone."

Julia was right about that. Elvis Karlsson really wants to be left alone. I intend to respect that and not try to force myself on him. But why on earth has he elected to hang around this house all the time? If I only knew the answer to that! Maybe it's because his mother's voice doesn't reach all the way here?

There is something else standing outside now— the man who is painting the house. I know who he is—I've seen him several times—he sometimes paints down at the beach. He doesn't only focus on houses about to be torn down, as Julia seems to think. She wants me to get rid of him, as I did the people who were here last week and tried to make off with the doors to the Dutch oven in the upper hallway. She is very suspicious of his motives!

The other day she came home, terribly upset. She had walked by an old house near her school just as it was about to be attacked by the bulldozers. They charged ahead, like monstrous lizards, and crushed everything in their path. They drove right into the walls, and the house collapsed as if it had been a house of cards.

There was a terrible roar, and then a terrible silence. There was a heavy, dusty smoke all over the place, and when it gradually floated away, nothing was left but the brick walls and the remains of the old Dutch oven on the upper floor. Now and then you could hear the clatter of bricks tumbling down from the walls.

Everything had happened terribly fast. One moment there was a big brown house, and the next, a pile of rubble. It looked as if a bomb had hit the place, or as if there had been an earthquake.

As Julia left the scene she saw "the man who was painting the house." But this time he wasn't painting. He had a camera on a tripod and was photographing the "demolition." He was completely absorbed in filming the horrible spectacle and didn't notice Julia. She was terribly upset. Why would he want to do a thing like that? How could he?

"He's probably one of those sadists," she said.

She reacted violently and was absolutely certain that the man belonged to the demolition gang. I tried to convince her that he was probably neither a sadist nor a member of the "gang." Maybe he paints and photographs houses about to be torn down to show people in this town how insane it is to destroy one beautiful old house after another. Many people understand this much better if it's represented by pictures; reality doesn't quite get to them.

Julia didn't believe me.

"It's true," I persisted. "Everyone is so used to looking at pictures in newspapers, and on television these days, that they don't accept it until they see it in picture form, which they understand better.

"Pictures are easier to understand than facts?" said Julia in amazement.

"Yes, that's the way it is these days," I said.

"I don't believe it," said Julia. She made it very plain that she didn't want to be contradicted. She still thinks that the artist is a villain. If we only could get rid of him, she feels, the house will be saved. But unfortunately it isn't that simple.

From all the phone calls I've made and letters I've written to the authorities, I've gathered that there are definite plans to tear this house down in order to make way for a number of row houses. But nothing is settled as yet, and I'm hoping that someone will pay attention to some of my letters. I tried to point out to the powers that be, that the city will lose its charm if they build row houses on the site of this garden, and that people will flee from the city if they destroy it in this way.

Besides, how do they know that anyone will want to live in their row houses? They will have a hard time renting them because the rents will be too high. Since they're tearing down so many other places, they could wait and see if they got people to move in before they build too many of those things and ruin the city.

We'll just have to hold on and see how things work out. . . .

JULIA

How I wish the stupid thing I'm going to tell had never happened!

Tryggve, our new teacher, brought a lot of records to school one day and played them in class. They were protest songs—all kinds of things —but as usual, Tryggve couldn't keep his mouth shut. To talk between the songs was one thing, but he kept on sounding like a stick stuck in a wheel all the way through. You couldn't hear a word of the lyrics, only Tryggve's voice going on and on. I was furious. Nothing makes me more irritated than when people say that now we're going to listen very carefully, and then they keep on babbling so you can't hear a single word. The whole thing was a total failure.

He had to explain what the songs meant, he said, although we could hear that ourselves. We do have ears, after all! It isn't necessary to understand every word; you get the meaning anyway—you kind of sense it. So his running commentary was completely wasted. I almost told him so—had it been anyone but Tryggve, I know that I wouldn't have been able to keep my mouth shut.

But now I didn't have the guts—not on account of Tryggve, but because of my classmates. I know what would have happened if I'd said anything. Tryggve has become one of those sacred cows. Everything he does is perfect. Can you believe it? You can't say a word against him. The girls have built him up to some kind of mystical figure by their blind admiration. The boys, however, are not so impressed.

"I'll kill you if you say anything against Tryggve!" Kerstin once said to me.

I wasn't going to say a thing. I guess I just looked a bit unenthusiastic when they were standing around making a fuss over him.

There's something weird about this Tryggve business. It's gone too far. The girls almost faint when he walks by. They worship him. It's like an

infectious disease that has spread from one to the
other. And although I think that Tryggve is cool
—he really is—he can't be compared to Peter.
Still, I'm a bit smitten by him.

But it affects me differently from the way it
does the others. It's hard for me to admit it because it sounds so silly. I join the gang when they
fall all over Tryggve because it's the easy way out.
It's a good feeling to be admiring somebody in a
group like that. If you don't have a best friend in
class, you don't care that much. It isn't so important. You're best friends with everyone if you dig
the same person. It's so hard to make good
friends, but then it's easy. You get lots of new
friends which you wouldn't have otherwise. . . .

If you dig Tryggve, you can be part of it—no
one gets left out.

That's why I've gone along with it; it's really
got nothing at all to do with Tryggve. I often
think mean thoughts about him, meaner than the
thoughts I think about anyone else I know, just
because it's forbidden. But of course I don't let
on. Instead I praise him. It's false and cowardly,
but I don't dare do anything else because of the
others.

It was the same thing now when he played
those records and just kept on running his mouth.

I felt like exploding during the whole hour, but at recess I didn't say a word. The madder I get at Tryggve, the more I praise him, and that's what I was doing now.

Suddenly Ulla looked at me and said: "You do like Tryggve better than Peter, don't you?"

I said I did. I didn't have a chance to think, so I just agreed. Ulla got one of those sensation-hungry looks in her eyes which she sometimes gets, and turned to Kerstin and Birgit.

"Did you hear that, girls?" she said. "She likes Tryggve better than her nightpa."

They nodded, trying to look important, and wearing a malicious and expectant expression. They sensed that I had made a fool of myself again, and thought this might be fun. I had really done a good job of it this time.

"Oh," said Ulla slowly, and a sly look came into her face. "That was the proof," she said, and paused.

The others didn't say anything. They just stood there waiting, and like an idiot, I did, too. I always freeze when Ulla gets started.

"It's because Peter isn't her real father that she can talk like that. I would never be able to say that I preferred someone else to my father. . . ."

"I couldn't either. . . ."

"Nor could I," said the others in unison, and looked at me.

"I didn't mean it that way," I began, but now it didn't matter what I said.

"What's said is said," said Kerstin.

I had said that I liked Tryggve more than Peter! Could I deny it? No, I couldn't possibly, they said.

"It's a good thing we found out!" said Ulla. Then she began whispering with the others, and I walked away. But they had a funny look on their faces for the rest of the day, and as soon as I came near them they said: "Well, now we know!"

I felt that they were up to something, and I was terrified, because with them you never know what's coming next. They might call Peter and tattle, or write him. They were capable of just about anything. . . .

When school was over I went straight home. I hurried because I wanted to call Peter and ask him to come earlier. I wanted to talk to him as soon as possible and explain everything.

But Mama was home; for once she wasn't in a hurry, and when she left I didn't get around to it. I had thought about what I was going to say, but by now I'd forgotten it; it was probably stupid anyway.

Instead I left the house; I didn't want to see
Peter. I couldn't face him, because even if Ulla
and the others hadn't had a chance to tell yet, the
fact remained that I had said it, and everyone had
heard me. It wasn't true, but that didn't make any
difference. What's said is said. Sooner or later
Peter would hear about it. He would never trust
me again. I had only raved about Tryggve to tease
him. This was my punishment and it served me
right. I was so terribly sad and so full of remorse,
but now it was too late. The only thing I could do
was to go away so that Peter wouldn't have to see
me. Then he might at least realize how sorry I was
for what I said. . . .

I didn't know where to go. My stomach was
churning. I thought of running to the hospital to
see Mama and tell her I had a pain in my appen-
dix and had to be admitted. But that wouldn't
work. . . .

I went down to the river. The boys who were
building the raft were there, so I sat down on a
hill a short distance away. It's a fine raft. It has a
bicycle right in the middle which works as a pro-
peller.

Åke and Bengt, the two boys who built it, were
talking about taking it out. But there was a third
guy with them down there. His name was Rolf,

and he kept pestering them about coming along, but the others refused. Finally Bengt and Åke walked away and took the oar with them. They probably got tired of listening to him.

Rolf stayed there for a while, but then he, too, disappeared. I went down to take a closer look at the raft, since the coast was clear. It lay tied up between a couple of stones with a rope which was attached to a tree.

Since it was very sturdy, I decided to climb on board. It must be the best raft ever built. They have painted it all sorts of colors and it's really beautiful, as big as a real boat.

In the middle of the raft there's a tent, and you can go inside and close the flap—which is what I did. I was only going to stay for a second because it was very cozy in there. That's when it happened.

Suddenly the float gave a lurch, and when I looked out from the tent, I saw that it was drifting away from the shore. It was going with the current so the speed was fantastic. I had no idea how it had happened.

Then I caught sight of Rolf standing on the shore laughing. It didn't take much to figure out that it was he who had untied the raft while I was inside the tent. Now he was standing there enjoying his mischief.

Suddenly he took off like lightning because he saw Bengt and Åke coming back; I heard their voices at a distance. When they got down to the river and saw what had happened, I was already quite far downstream. They were furious because they naturally thought it was my fault, and they screamed and jumped up and down in their rage and frustration.

I didn't answer—I was too far away. I was sure they would kill Rolf if they found out he did it. But in any case, I was beyond their reach.

I was sick and tired of everything. I had no place to go, and I might as well drift out to sea on this raft. At least it was exciting while it lasted, and it wasn't dangerous. The raft was like a floating island. I got on the bicycle and began pedaling, and was really enjoying myself.

The boys were far behind and didn't bother me. The town looked pretty, seen from the river —dreamlike and unreal with budding trees and shimmering grass. White gulls were flying overhead. What a mass of sky the birds have to fly around in!

A hare was chasing a lot of crows from his nest

in a field. The crows, usually so noisy, were strangely quiet; they were probably disappointed that they didn't find anything to eat. As I floated by, I tried to help the rabbit by screaming as much as I could at the crows so that they scattered in different directions.

I was beginning to feel quite contented and to feel that somehow everything would turn out all right with Peter, and with the house, which really

gets me down. I somehow knew that it would all work out. It has to, because the world is a fine and beautiful place, and you see it when you float along at a distance like this; you see nothing ugly or bad.

It's a fantastic sensation to be bicycling on the water. I even began to whistle, although I don't know how, unfortunately. But when I'm happy, I always want to and then only a sound like "fjtt" comes out. Peter has tried to teach me, but it's hopeless. I have no talent for whistling, but this time I thought I sounded better than usual.

Just then I heard a whistle from the shore! Much louder than mine! A whistle that I knew so well! And there was Peter!

He was cycling also, but on land. He looked all in. He was waving to me and pedaling for all he was worth.

"Don't be afraid! I'm coming! Just keep calm," he repeated, gasping for breath.

But I was calm. I wasn't afraid at all, but Peter didn't seem to understand that. He just kept on pedaling and got more and more out of breath. The road was bad, so sometimes he had to jump off the bicycle and run alongside it. I felt terribly sorry for him. It was obvious that he was frantically worried about me, and I couldn't even reassure him because he wasn't listening. As soon as I tried to say something, he would shout, "Just keep calm. I'm coming!"

We were approaching the big bridge which spans the river in a high arc from one shore to the other. A man was fishing at the foot of the bridge. I saw that I would be floating by the old man at a close range, and I didn't like the idea, because he might start asking a lot of questions, especially if Peter kept on shouting like that.

That's why I looked away as I came under the bridge, but that didn't help a bit. The man must have been gunning his motor because he immediately set off towards the raft. He thought I was in distress and he was just being helpful, but I wasn't the least bit happy when he rescued me.

He turned off the motor and told me to climb into his boat. We were right under the bridge.

"It's all right," I said. "I'm in no danger."

He didn't pay any attention to me but just grabbed me and got me into the boat. There was nothing I could do. Everything had gone wrong, and he didn't care about the beautiful raft—he just let it float downstream.

I should have said something, but I was too confused. We were just coming out from under the bridge when I saw Peter up on it. He had his back turned and didn't see us. We had gotten to the other side of the bridge. The float was still under it.

I was frightened out of my wits. Peter had climbed over the railing and was standing up there swaying, and I didn't get my mouth open to call out before he let go and dove into the water. And disappeared. Just as the raft appeared from under the bridge. He couldn't see that it was empty. Or else maybe he thought that I had crawled into the tent. Otherwise he probably wouldn't have jumped in.

I said to the old man that we had to pick up Peter too, but he just headed for a small boat-landing on the beach.

"That stupid idiot will have to take care of himself," he said, glancing indifferently over his shoulder in Peter's direction.

It was unbelievable! But that's the way people's minds work. They just don't think things out. It didn't matter what I said, he just kept on laughing and thought he was being clever.

"With children it's a different matter," he said. "Children are children, but a grown man who jumps in the river has only himself to blame."

He was so convinced he was right that it was impossible to reason with him.

Peter had emerged on the surface of the water and was trying to swim to the raft. As we reached the boat-landing, I saw that he had made it. The old man put me ashore and I ran as fast as I could so that Peter would see me and not think that I had drowned, calling out to him all the time.

But he didn't hear me—the raft was too far away. He must have been exhausted because he was lying on the deck catching his breath, hardly moving.

I ran up on the bridge and grabbed the bicycle which he had left there. I started to cycle along the shore, but couldn't catch up with the raft. Peter was on his way out to sea. I was terrified. There were no people in sight.

I stopped and called out to Peter. No answer. Then I called for help. Still no answer. Only silence, except for screeching seagulls. The only thing left for me to do was to ride back to town and get help.

But Peter has to tell the rest. . . .

PETER

JULIA ASKED ME to tell what happened when I floated out to sea, so I'll begin from the beginning.

It was the day I came late to her house because I had to wait for a long-distance call at home. I was about twenty minutes late, and then I stopped and bought some apple cake at the bakery on the square, and that also took some time.

When I arrived I went straight to the kitchen to make tea. Julia wasn't around, but the house is big and I thought she was busy with something. I set the table and then sat down to read the paper while I waited, expecting her to show up any minute.

It was a beautiful day. The windows were open, and the wonderful smells of bird cherry and other blooming shrubbery wafted through the room and mingled with the smell of tea. I was feeling good, and happy that I had bought six apple cakes so that we could have three each.

Then, suddenly, I heard excited voices from the river. It sounded as if there was trouble down there. My first impulse was to shut the window so that I didn't have to hear it, but instead I just stood there listening. In an instant my happy mood was gone, and I was filled with a feeling of anxiety.

Why wasn't Julia here? Were they calling her name down there? It sounded like it to me. I ran around the house looking for her and calling her, but there was no answer. The commotion down at the river continued. If she was down there, she was in some kind of trouble; that much I sensed.

I ran down to the river. There were the boys who had built the raft. They were furious and didn't calm down when they saw me. They glared at me and tried to outshout each other, claiming that Julia had taken their raft and made off with

it. But I know her well enough to know that such
an idea would never have occurred to her.

"Someone else must have done it," I said.

But they were positive it was Julia; they had
seen her with their own eyes. They had gone
home to fetch a figurehead for the raft, and had
taken the steering oar along just to be sure, because there was a guy who wanted to go with
them on the raft but they didn't want him along.
They had seen Julia up on the hill watching
them, but hadn't thought there was any risk that
she—a girl—would touch their raft, and they
knew that the other guy wouldn't take it with the
steering oar gone. A boy wouldn't be that stupid,
they added.

"Neither is Julia," I said.

That made them even more furious. She had
been just that stupid, they said. When they came
back with the figurehead, the raft was gone. And
when they looked down the river, there it was,
floating away, with Julia on board. They screamed
and yelled at her, but she just sat there calmly,
not even bothering to answer.

"But the other guy, where was he?"

There was no sign of him, they said. That
meant she was alone.

I realized that they were telling the truth, but it was hard to grasp because it was completely unlike Julia to do a thing like that.

I became terribly worried. The raft was solid and well built, but she didn't have a steering oar. She would float out to sea if she wasn't stopped in time. She was helpless.

The guys were standing there with their figurehead and their oar, glaring at me. The figurehead was an old head from a display dummy which one of the boys had gotten from his aunt, who had a hat shop. All it needed was a bit of paint. I just stood there staring at it, as if I thought it might give me some help. But it didn't, and I had to take action. I promised the boys that they would get their raft back in perfect condition, and left. I took the bike and started off along the shore.

It was quite a while before I caught sight of the raft. Julia was on board. She was sitting on the bicycle and pedaling. God, how terribly sorry I felt for her! Poor kid! She was obviously struggling to get to shore. She probably thought that everything would be all right if she pedaled hard enough, and that the raft was as easy to manage as a bicycle.

I called to her not to be afraid, and that I was coming, but I realized that she was too out of

breath to answer. I was terribly out of breath myself. She shouted something, but I couldn't hear her. She continued to pedal but was obviously at the end of her strength.

Soon she would be drifting out to sea—and she didn't have far to go. But first she had to pass under the bridge. My plan was to get up on the bridge before the raft got there, wait until the right moment, and as it floated by, jump into the water and climb aboard. If I could manage to get up on it I could pry loose a plank, which would serve as a steering oar to maneuver us to shore.

Everything would have worked out if other people hadn't run interference. I got up on the bridge just as the raft was going under the opposite side from where I was standing, but I jumped and landed right behind it. It took a bit of doing to catch up with it, but I managed.

When I had finally climbed up on the raft, I found it empty. Julia was no longer on board. It was a terrible shock. Besides, I was all in after the bicycle ride and then the swim. For a while I lay there like a dead fish, hardly able to move a fin. But then I jumped up as terror filled me again. Where was Julia? Had she fallen overboard and drowned?

Then to my incredible relief I saw her far, far away. She was cycling along the shore. She was alive and safe! What a miracle! I was so relieved that I lay down again, thinking I would have a few moments' rest before I started ripping up boards for steering oars.

But that I shouldn't have done.

There isn't much more to tell. The story has a sorry ending. I fell asleep on the raft. I was warm and comfortable, the sun was still shining and the weather was calm. My clothes were sopping wet, but the sun warmed them. I felt as if I were in a hot compress, and that made me very drowsy—probably why I fell asleep.

I didn't wake up until I was far out at sea. Screeching seagulls and human voices awakened me. I had no idea where I was, and honestly, I was scared to death. A lot of kids were water skiing around me, and in the boats that were circling around, people were gaping and shouting funny remarks to each other.

"The guy seems all in!"

"Yes, he has his exercycle on board."

It wasn't a very pleasant awakening. I didn't know which way to turn, but felt like crawling into the tent and hiding. Then I saw a boat coming directly towards me. Someone was sitting on the prow, waving. It was Julia! She was coming to save me. But of course she wasn't alone. A policeman whom she had found in town was with her. When he heard what had happened, he immediately got into action and arranged for a boat—a large one that could tow the raft, so that it could be delivered to the boys in perfect condition, which is what I had promised.

The ending certainly wasn't what I had expected. I was going to be the one who saved Julia, but now, wide awake, I didn't feel exactly like a hero, being towed by the police boat. I was also shivering because the sun was going down. Julia saw that I was cold, and asked the policeman to give me a blanket. She wrapped it around me, settled herself next to me, and took my hand.

"You're not very practical, Peter," she said seriously. "As a matter of fact, you're terribly impractical."

"What do you mean?" I said, stupefied.

I didn't consider myself impractical at all. Everything would have gone off as I had planned it, if that old man hadn't fished Julia out. But Julia shook her head, looked very concerned, and let go my hand.

"First you jump from the bridge and into the water," she said. "Then you lie down and fall asleep—and let the raft drift off wherever it wants to!"

I thought that one over, but couldn't agree with her. Aside from the fact that it was idiotic to lie down and fall asleep, I felt I had done what the situation called for.

"What do you think I should have done?" I asked.

Julia gestured toward the police boat. "That's what you should have done," she said gently.

Of course. Unfortunately, I had to admit that I would never have thought about that myself. I sighed, whereupon she took my hand and tried to console me.

"That's because you like to be dramatic," she said, "and I like that."

I think she meant it.

When we had returned the raft and were back home, and finally sat down to drink fresh tea, because the old was cold, and eat the apple cakes, I was forced to drink hot milk with honey so that I wouldn't catch a cold. I tried to get out of it, but Julia had a will of iron.

"Now you're being impractical again," she said. "But then you won't get any tea, and no apple cake either!"

All I could do was to obey.

Then Julia told me what had happened, and how she had come to be on the raft. Of course I had known all along that it hadn't been her idea to take off like that.

But then, after thinking for a moment, she said that she wasn't innocent after all, because she hadn't done a thing to stop the raft. She had wanted to go out to sea, to go away as far as possible.

"I had decided not to see you anymore," she said.

"In heaven's name why?" I said, startled.

Then she told me that she had "betrayed" me.

"How?" I said, because she made it sound quite serious.

At first she wouldn't talk, but finally she confessed that she had said to Ulla and her gang that she liked Tryggve better than me. It wasn't at all true, she said, because Tryggve was a phony, but what is said can't be unsaid.

"Is that all?" I said. "You didn't betray me by that remark. What nonsense! Now *you* are being dramatic!"

I tried to explain to her that I didn't feel in the least bit betrayed because she preferred other people to me. Not even if I had been her own father would I have been hurt, because all people mean different things to each other, and can't be compared. She mustn't have a bad conscience about that, I said.

This pleased her a great deal.

"But I still like you best of all," she said.

"That's good to know in case someone else should turn up," I said.

"That's impossible!" exclaimed Julia.

Then we talked about Tryggve. It went all right this time, and I didn't get that dusty feeling in my throat.

"Tryggve can be quite a pain sometimes," said Julia, and began to recite a list of his faults. That made him quite human—in fact I began to think of him as quite nice, and found myself sitting there defending Tryggve as if he had been my own brother.

Then Julia flared up. "I've had it!" she exclaimed. "I thought I was pleasing you, and now you praise him the way the others do. That's the limit!"

"It couldn't possibly please me that you put Tryggve down," I said. "I don't understand what you're getting at."

She really lashed out at me. But I know that she understood what I meant, because in the middle she broke off and said:

"That's true, because it doesn't help me if you say nasty things about Ulla. But even if you did, I could never defend her. That I would never do!"

"But you don't have to," I said.

"Then why do you defend Tryggve?"

I didn't have a chance to answer, because suddenly she looked terribly worried.

"Maybe you're catching cold after all. You probably have a fever. That's why you're being so noble," she said.

I assured her that nothing was wrong with me, but to no avail, I had to down another cup of hot milk with honey before Julia would calm down. I wouldn't ever dare to defend Tryggve again!

That ends the adventure with the raft.

I still haven't heard a word from the authorities as to what is going to happen to the house, and that bothers me. Julia isn't asking questions. I realize that she is leaving everything in my hands, and that she is depending on me to solve the problem. But every day I get more worried.

To end this chapter, though, I have to report that Elvis Karlsson is making progress—he is becoming quite bold. He really amazes me.

The other day I happened to be standing looking out of the window in the upper hall, when I saw Elvis coming towards the garden gate. He had a paper swallow in his hand. For a long time he stood absolutely still. Then he looked around and quickly threw his paper swallow over the gate into the garden. It was very clear that he had done it deliberately, and either he has strong arms or else he had a favorable wind, because the swallow landed in the middle of the garden.

Then he stood as still as before; he seemed to be waiting and watching for something to happen. He looked around quickly before opening the gate and running into the garden.

He didn't immediately retrieve his swallow, as I thought he would, but prowled around the garden, stopping and looking from time to time. For quite a while he stood gazing at the flower bed in front of the steps leading to the kitchen. He also stopped in front of the cellar door, and below Julia's window.

Then he quickly ran to fetch his swallow, ran through the gate and disappeared.

What was he after? Did he launch that swallow to have an excuse to come inside the gate? What would he have done if someone had come out? He must at least have considered that as a possibility. Maybe he even hoped to meet someone—but in that case, whom?

JULIA

I JUST KNOW that Peter is going to save the house, so I'm not worried, although it gives me a creepy feeling to see that man hanging around painting pictures of it. Now I can prove that he has something to do with tearing it down. He doesn't only paint the houses before they are destroyed, but during the process he stands there filming the whole thing. I've seen it with my own eyes. Can you imagine anything so creepy?

I happened to be walking by just as they were tearing a house down. It was one of the most awful things I've seen. It was so sad I couldn't even cry; I don't even want to write about it.

I wanted to run away, but my legs became

paralyzed and I couldn't seem to move. Lots of people were standing around watching.

A ghastly thought came into my head, so ghastly that I can hardly express it, but I started to think about executions. First they condemn a house, they decide on the day, and then the bulldozer comes like an executioner. There's no chance to plead for mercy. The bulldozer just keeps on coming closer and closer and then attacks.

When a house is condemned it's the end.

I couldn't help thinking about our house, although I tried not to, and it made me feel terrible.

When it was all over I saw the man. I recognized him immediately, but he didn't see me. He had a camera and was photographing the sad sight —or filming it; I don't know which. That's why I think there's something wrong with him. There's got to be, because who would choose to take pictures of destruction? You take pictures to remember, but what is there to remember about this? That's what I don't understand.

But the most awful thing about it was that when I came home, there he was, painting the outside of our house! He must have come directly here.

I had an eerie sensation, because when the picture is finished, the bulldozer will be here—that was all too clear to me. Peter claims that it makes no sense at all, and Mama too, but they can say what they like—the only time I worry about the house is when that man stands here painting it. Otherwise I rely on Peter.

When I saw him right after the demolition, I almost fainted. I stopped to watch him from a distance, and then thought of sneaking away so that he wouldn't see me. But then the idea struck me that I might be able to keep him from finishing his painting of the house, and that if I did, it would put off its being torn down. After all, I also have to do my best, and not always count on others.

So I walked up to him. He didn't look at me because he was painting a window, but he was friendly.

"Hi, how are you?" he said.

"Terrible," I answered.

"Same here," he said. "I can't get the light right."

"What?"

"The glitter in the window is hard to capture."

126

"Is it?"

"Yes, but it's a good feeling when you succeed. . . ."

Finally he looked at me.

The strange part about it is that he has kind eyes, although they look sad, as if he didn't want to do what he was doing, but had to, in spite of himself. I realize that he doesn't have to be a bad person—he can be good—but he seems to be the victim of fate; that is, he does things that have already been decided. That's even more dangerous in a way, because he isn't responsible for what he does, and that's a spooky thought. But there is something strange about him, and you can tell by his voice, because he almost whispers.

I had planned my strategy; I was going to be polite, well-mannered but a bit foxy, so I said that the picture was good, which it was. He was quite far along on the house, although there was still a lot to be done.

When they build real houses they start from the bottom, from the foundation, but he had started from the top with the roof. I suppose it's different when you paint.

It looked weird, this half house floating on air, a ghost house, romantic, and a bit scary.

At first he didn't answer when I said that the painting was good. But after a while he said:

"I don't know . . . I'm not quite satisfied with it yet. . . ."

"When will it be finished?"

"Well, I shouldn't think it would take much longer."

That put terror into me, but I tried not to

show it. I looked around the garden and saw lots of things that he hadn't painted—that he had just skipped over. The trees were also quite sloppily painted, and I told him so, but he only laughed.

"The house is the most important part, isn't it? I don't think I'll do much about the rest."

I thought that was stupid reasoning, because the garden will also disappear.

"But isn't that just as important?" I asked.

He nodded and said that I was probably right. He would have to do a bit more about the garden than he had planned.

"But one thing at a time. First the house," he insisted.

That was exactly what I didn't want! I had to think of something else.

"The garden is at its best right now," I said. "Soon the tulips won't be in bloom, and the narcissus . . ."

"After that something else will bloom," he said calmly. "Besides, too much would spoil it. I already have the chestnut in full bloom, and I think that's just about enough. . . ."

"But you couldn't ever have enough flowers!" I exclaimed, because I thought what he said sounded crazy.

"On paintings you can," he said.

I don't agree, because if he is going to paint things the way they are, then he ought to do it. But he didn't feel that way about it. He is a very stubborn man and paints only what he wants to paint; he made that very clear. And he knew exactly what he wanted.

It looked hopeless. I pointed out the garden furniture, and the bench under the weeping birch, and the table with the marble top, and all sorts of things—things that other people love in our garden.

But he just shook his head. There was no hurry, the furniture would be there as long as the house was still standing, he said. He still hadn't quite decided what he was going to include in the picture.

There seemed to be no way of making him change his mind. Finally I ran out of ideas. As he stubbornly kept on painting the house—now he was doing another window—I felt myself getting more and more depressed. Then suddenly I got a fantastic idea!

"What do you like to paint best?" I asked.

"I don't know," he mused. "The light, perhaps; it's always changing; it's exciting. . . ."

"Is that why you like to paint windows?"

He said he thought that might be it.

"Then it must also be exciting to paint water also?"

"Yes," he said, "that might also be fun."

I kept still for a while, and then I asked:

"Then why don't you paint the puddles?"

It had been raining the whole day and the path and the ground in front of the entrance were filled with unusually beautiful puddles.

He stopped painting, but he didn't say a word. He just stood there staring at the garden, and the hand that held the brush fell to his side.

"The water puddles won't be there as long as the house," I added.

He still didn't say anything, but that was O.K., because he didn't say no the way he did before. He just kept on staring ahead of him, and I could tell he was thinking about it.

I can't remember ever having seen such beautiful puddles. Some were dark and mysterious-looking—they were a shimmering greenish-black —probably the reflection of the trees. Then there were some that glittered like silver or gold, and some were almost white or pale pink, like mother-of-pearl. They were beautiful in a strange way, and that instant I was struck by how they transformed the whole garden into a magical place.

He probably saw it too, although he still didn't say anything. After a while he put his brush down and began squeezing paint out of the tubes.

"What colors are those?" I wanted to know.

He told me their names, but they were so strange I immediately forgot them.

After a while I asked: "What are you going to do with those colors?"

"Paint the puddles, of course," he said. "As you said, one never knows how long they're going to last."

"Then you're not going to paint the house anymore?"

"Not today in any case," he said. "I'll be happy if I can manage to do those puddles."

"They'll probably take a very long time."

"I'm afraid so."

"Now you can paint light reflections as much as you like."

The idea seemed to appeal to him, but he didn't say anything. He was probably thinking about how he was going to go about it, because puddles are probably very difficult to paint. I thought it was just as well to leave him alone.

"So long," I said.

He nodded and said good-bye, but he didn't look in my direction because he had already started to paint. He seemed to be quite pleased.

I certainly was! Terribly pleased! Now at least I, too, have done something for the house, and not just waited for Peter to do everything. And I think we've gained a little time. . . .

PETER

THE HOUSE IS definitely going to be torn down. Now it's a fact.

Julia's mother just called and told me. She has received a letter informing her that they have found her an apartment—two rooms in a modern building. She was told to prepare to move out as soon as possible, as the house was next on the demolition list.

She didn't sound happy, but said that she had to make the best of it. The problem was Julia— she hadn't told her and wanted me to do it.

I understood why. I've been far too optimistic. I've led Julia to believe that the house could be saved. I honestly thought so myself. Of course I had my moments of doubt, but I never dreamed that things would turn out this way. The authorities have obviously ignored my letters and phone calls. I wonder if they'll even bother to answer me.

When you come down to it, I'm responsible for how Julia is going to take this. I'll be going over there in a while and then I'll have to tell her.

If only there were something I could do! I don't like to be a troublemaker, but should I stand by and watch this happen? Isn't there something seriously wrong here? Those in power shouldn't be sitting around making decisions without consulting those who are affected. They ought to be thinking what is best for the town, and the people who live here. Since so many feel that the city will become an ugly and dull place if they carry through their program, they ought to listen to what the people say, and give it some thought.

Things haven't been going well for this urban renewal project. And if they continue without paying attention to people, things might get worse. Isn't it high time that they stop and reconsider before it's too late? But it seems that the only way to get their attention is to cause trouble.

I find myself getting angrier by the minute, and when you feel that way you can't think sensibly. If I try to keep cool, perhaps I'll come up with a new idea. Right now I'll think about Elvis Karlsson instead.

One day last week he showed up here with a ball—a red ball. He was standing there with it in the same place I saw him the last time—outside the gate. He wasn't playing; he just stood there holding the ball in his hands as if he were getting ready for something. And sure enough! After a while he aimed and threw it into the garden.

Exactly the same thing happened as the last time; he didn't even bother to pretend it was a mistake. The ball didn't land too far away from him. He waited for a while before he opened the gate and went in. I expected him to run around the garden again, but he didn't. He just picked up the ball and left.

Outside the gate he stopped. He had probably missed his aim, because he tried again, this time throwing the ball with all his might. It landed farther away than before, but not much. I could tell that he wasn't satisfied this time either. He shook his head as he ambled off to fetch it. He tried a third time and put all his effort into it, but that was still worse. The ball landed only a few feet away. He isn't very good at this—I think he probably holds onto the ball too long.

After the third attempt he gave up, picked up his ball and left.

But after a while he was back again, and this time he had the paper swallow with him. There was something purposeful and determined about him. It was obvious that he had something in mind.

I was curious because I sensed that something was about to happen, and placed myself so that I would have a view over the garden without being seen.

Elvis was standing down at the gate, deep in thought, taking his time. He made sure that no one was looking, then threw the swallow and waited. I thought the swallow flew quite a distance, but Elvis apparently wasn't satisfied, because he immediately ran to fetch it.

He spent some time fussing with it before he sent it up again, and this time it made a long-distance flight and landed right next to the house —under Julia's window in a flower bed where bluebells had recently been in bloom.

After standing around and waiting as usual, Elvis opened the gate and went into the garden. He didn't hurry, didn't run as before, but walked with deliberate steps, all the while fishing in the pocket of his jacket for something. He kept on digging so that it was a wonder the pocket survived, but he never came up with anything. When he reached the swallow, he again stopped and looked thoughtful. He bent down and studied the ground around it, but he didn't touch it. Instead he picked up a bit of soil, felt it with his fingers, and smelled it. Then he got down on his knees, picked up the swallow, and poked around in the ground where it had lain. He lay there digging for quite a while, apparently not concerned about whether anyone saw him. Julia would be coming along any minute. What would he do then?

But no Julia, and Elvis took his time. When he had finished poking around in the ground, he dug in his pocket again and came up with a crumpled paper bag, which he smoothed out and emptied into his hand. Unfortunately, I couldn't see what it was, but he looked at it carefully and smelled it. Then he quickly bent down, I couldn't see what he was doing, but I think he put something in the soil, because I saw him flatten it with the palm of his hand. Finally he took a stick and wrote something on the ground.

He seemed to have finished whatever he was

doing because he took his paper swallow and walked away backwards, his eyes glued on the small spot where he had been digging.

Just as he closed the gate, I saw Julia coming. How lucky that she hadn't come earlier! She was walking on the other side of the street and didn't see Elvis until the moment they met. They had almost passed each other when they said hello. That was a surprise to me. I didn't hear Elvis respond, but he made a gesture. He didn't nod the way others do, but in a funny way nodded backwards, and then immediately looked away.

That was the first time I had ever seen him greet anyone.

When Julia came in that afternoon I didn't mention it, but the first moment I had, I slipped out to see what he had been up to.

It wasn't hard to find the spot where he had been digging. The ground was smooth and flattened, and on top he had drawn a sun with lots of rays around it. But I still had no idea what he had buried there. The sun seemed to be a kind of protection. If it hadn't been for that, I could probably have poked around, but now it was impossible without damaging his sun. Elvis Karlsson knew what he was doing.

Later I became convinced that he'd hidden

something there, because after that, he came back every day to check that the sun hadn't been touched. And if it had rained, he patched it up. He always brought the swallow along; it's part of the whole thing, because he always threw it in first. I wonder if I'll ever find out what's hidden in the ground under Elvis Karlsson's sun?

But that was a week ago, and now it's time to go to Julia and tell her the truth.

Later. I'm at Julia's now. She is not at home now, but she was when I arrived. She had made

tea, which we drank, and everything was as usual.

She asked me why I was so quiet, and I told her exactly how things stood. Maybe that was all wrong. Perhaps I should have broken the news in easy stages.

"I'm terribly sorry, Julia, but everything went down the drain. I wasn't able to prevent it—the house is definitely coming down. They notified us. . . ."

At first she didn't say a word. She just stared at me and turned terribly pale.

I told her that her mother had called, and that they would get a modern apartment instead. She still didn't open her mouth, just kept on staring. I said that I had done the best I could, I had tried with all my might, but it was obviously not enough. The authorities had paid no attention to what I said. They just decided according to what was in their own heads—way above ours. I had hoped that I'd be able to change their thinking, but I had failed.

"I can't tell you how sorry I am, Julia. I ought to have known. . . ."

But I had the feeling that she was looking at me without seeing me. I no longer knew what to say. There was no point in repeating what she already knew, so I kept quiet.

Then she got up from the table and glared at me.

"You promised," was all she said, and walked towards the door. She stopped for a moment and again fixed her eyes on me.

"You promised!" she repeated, and her eyes were black.

I didn't say anything. What was there to say?

She closed the door behind her, and I heard her go out. I didn't go after her. It was hard not to, but she had to be alone now.

JULIA

BEFORE PETER HAD SAID a word I knew that the house was going to be torn down. I knew, because the picture was finished. The evening before, I had met the artist when he came from here—he was carrying the picture under his arm. He stopped and asked if I wanted to look at it—he had just finished it.

But I didn't want to, so I walked away. But then I regretted it, because I thought that I might be able to find something on the house which he hadn't finished. I went back and looked very carefully, but he hadn't left anything out.

He had skipped a couple of tulips in front of the house, which would have made it too cluttered—the picture, that is—but not in real life. Instead, he had painted a sunflower under my window. It's beautiful; it doesn't exist in reality, but it doesn't matter because I like sunflowers, so it was a good idea.

"What made you think of doing that?" I asked.

He said that it was a secret, so he couldn't tell me.

It's probably the most beautiful picture in the world, but so sad, because everything that's on it is going to disappear—except for the sunflower, because that doesn't exist, and never has, and that's probably just as well for its sake.

"Now the bulldozer will probably come any minute," I said.

"Isn't that the damnedest thing you ever heard?" (I'm writing exactly what he said, because I could tell that he meant it, and I agree with him!)

After a while I said: "You shouldn't have finished painting the house."

He shrugged his shoulders and asked what difference that made. He looked terribly sad, and I no longer think it's his fault. As Peter says, there are others who decide, and they never show their faces.

But how can their decision count if they are

never around? They just invent something to decide and then disappear into thin air—that's a pretty scary thought, isn't it? And when you never get to see the people who do all these stupid things, you get mad and blame other people who didn't have anything to do with it, and are only trying to do their best. That man, for instance. It's all right that he paints all the houses that are going to be torn down. Now I understand that it's so that later they can see everything they've destroyed. Otherwise they'll forget what they've done and tell themselves that what they did was good.

Yes, I already knew when Peter told me, but maybe I didn't believe it, after all, because up until then I had been able to control myself, although it had been churning around in my mind all the time.

But when he told me, I cracked, and I was even more miserable because it was Peter. I had been counting so much on him.

I still do. But at that moment everything went to pieces and I was thinking the most awful thoughts. I told myself that I would never depend on anyone again, because people aren't made so that they can depend on each other. And I'm not either.

People seem destined to disappoint each other, and then to have to harden themselves against each other. But now that I was hardened I would never be fooled again, because I was through with trusting people forever.

But luckily those thoughts went away quickly. I've noticed that the most awful thoughts go away the quickest. That's probably because you don't have the strength to drag them around too long, and that's a good thing.

Now I trust Peter more than ever before. He wanted to help, and he tried. He really believed that he would be able to handle those people, and as long as he believed it, we were happy. But he did all he could, and it wasn't his fault that he couldn't reach them. And when it didn't work out he told the truth and didn't blame anyone else—that's something he would never do.

He was sad; it showed all over him.

But I have to cheer up. Otherwise he will feel even worse, and I will too, which will make him even sadder, and then we'll both give up. We mustn't let that happen.

But when I first knew for sure what was about to happen, I couldn't think, because there was a roar in my head; it sounded like thunder, and after that everything stopped. I had to go out.

I must have been away quite a while, because it was dark when I came back, and Smuggler was there. Peter was wearing his black earmuffs, which he always does when Smuggler tries to feed him through the ears.

I felt rotten because I had been so mean, so I walked up to Peter.

"You did promise," I said, "but it doesn't matter...."

I was going to say more, but there was no point in it because of those earmuffs, and besides, we both burst into laughter because Smuggler was being impossible. He kept on fluttering around our heads, trying to start a commotion. He acts that way sometimes. And although we took out our water pistols and slingshots to calm him down, he only became wilder. He seemed to be having a very good time.

Then Peter aimed his water pistol at me and made my hair all wet.

"This is for you because you can't understand that it's possible to fail," he said.

Then I shot him with a pea.

"And that's for you because you can't understand that people can be furious, and then sorry afterwards!"

He laughed, and so did I. There was nothing

more to say. All those stupid things were behind us, and we both felt it.

When I think about it, Peter never did promise that the house wouldn't be torn down as I had said. He only promised to try to prevent it. But that didn't occur to me until now—my thinking seems to be kind of slow.

The same night, when Smuggler had calmed down and was swinging in the chandelier and we were playing Peter's strange, mystical records, with only one small light burning, Peter suddenly looked around. It was almost as if he were near-sighted and couldn't see me.

"So there you are! You look so tiny," he said.

"I do?"

"Yes, and when it really comes down to it, you're probably too small for this house."

That made me look around, too.

The ceilings are very high, and there are shadows everywhere, although I like shadows. Then I looked at Peter and he also looked pretty small, much smaller than the shadows. I said that in that case, he was also too small. And Smuggler, too.

"It's really a house for a lot of people," I said. Peter flew out of his chair so that the light flickered.

"Julia!" he cried. "You've got something there!"

Then he explained what he meant. If we suggest that they give this house to the town, so that people would have a place to meet, they might not tear it down, he said, because the city owns it, and such a place is needed. There have been several articles in the newspapers about that.

It's a great idea, and those in command should be able to understand.

Peter promised to write to them right away, so that they would have the letter tomorrow. They can't say no. Now that they have a wonderful suggestion about how to save the house for everybody to enjoy, they just have to say yes!

We were terribly excited when we had that idea, because the house is really pretty big for Mama and me, even though Peter and Smuggler are here part of the time. I'm thinking of people who have to crowd into one room and don't have anywhere to go. Then everyone who feels crowded at home, or alone, or bored, could come here and meet friends, and make new ones.

It's too bad that we didn't think of this before. Peter thinks so too. But we were being selfish and thinking only of ourselves. And I don't think the thought would ever have crossed our minds if we hadn't found out that they were going to tear the house down. Peter doesn't think so either.

Isn't it awful to be that selfish? Even though it's hard for me to think about it, maybe what is happening is good, in a certain way. But those "authorities" were still dumb, for how could they know that we would come up with this great idea?

The most important thing is, not that we live in this house, but that it be saved! If it were for everybody, we could also come here as much as we wanted to! When it belongs to everyone, it will be Peter's and mine, too, and not the property of those unseen authorities!

I'm beginning to feel that everything will turn out all right for everyone. And so does Peter. I'm so happy that I probably won't sleep a wink. . . .

I open the window. The moon is shining and summer is here.

There's a light in Peter's room, so he isn't sleeping either. He's probably sitting there working on that letter. . . .

PETER

Nothing seems to be working out.

Julia and I had the idea that this house could become a meeting place so that people in this town would have somewhere to go. I wrote a long letter to the authorities and presented the case, suggesting that it be a "club for social activities," so that they would take me seriously. It's important that you use the right (i.e., their) words. Those in power like complicated words for simple things, so that people won't get the idea that any problem is simple and obvious.

But the decision to tear the house down was

final. There was no possibility of changing that.

"Nonsense. They're only trying to act important," Julia said. "As long as the house is still standing, it can't be too late, can it?"

I agreed that it was a lot of nonsense. Was there any reason why stupid decisions couldn't be reversed? There's nothing wrong with changing one's mind. But some people seem to think so. Only children turn over a new leaf without being ashamed—not grown-ups, and certainly not those who decide things. They think so highly of themselves that there's no room for improvement.

I don't agree with them. And there are more and more people around town who are beginning to doubt their judgment.

They say the bulldozer will come here next week.

If they've set the date, they haven't notified anyone as yet—not even Julia's mother. All she knows is that she has to hurry. She is a cooperative lady, and has already started to pack.

Julia and I aren't that obedient—we have other plans.

They may want to speed up the destruction to get the whole thing over with. Afterwards they can blame one another, or else say, "What's done is done."

Those are magic words and can't be contradicted. They stop all further questions.

"How childish," says Julia. "That's the way Ulla and her gang reason: What's done is done, and what's been said can't be unsaid."

So therefore Julia and I have been going around talking to people about how this house can be put to use, so that everyone will benefit from it.

The artist who painted the house has done a good deed. He has put the painting on display in the bookshop at the square, and has printed in large letters above it: THIS HOUSE IS ALSO GOING TO BE TORN DOWN.

There are always people standing in front of the painting. Many of them come and ask to see the house, and of course they are welcome. They walk around in here and can't understand how anyone can have the insane idea of tearing down such a beautiful, spacious and well-built old house as this. The garden that surrounds it is like a park. How can they even think of destroying it! And for what? To build row houses!

Of course the building is a bit dilapidated and needs a few repairs, but many people are ready to help if only we can save the house. Nobody wants it torn down, and nobody wants row houses here.

This time around, most people are wise to what the authorities mean when they say what's done is done. They would have a hard time explaining. People are beginning to remember all the other houses that have disappeared. And when they see what has replaced them they have started to think.

Some want to start a protest movement. They say they're going to stop the bulldozer when it comes.

But Julia and I have a better idea.

Our plan hinges on finding out what day the demolition is going to start. I gather it's very soon, because the guy in charge is constantly snooping around here.

He also brings a crowd with him. Once when Julia and I came home, the house was full of all kinds of people walking around and examining everything. These people have no objection to the house being torn down—on the contrary. They're here to buy up everything of value to put in their own houses. But they're not allowed to cart it away as yet, so there are strange names in big red letters on most things—floors, panels, doors, and window frames. On Dutch ovens and wardrobes, and even on the kitchen stove, there are names such as Jonsson, Berg, Lund, Carlsson, etc., written in big red letters.

Such people exist, too. It's a good thing we don't know any of them. They probably aren't from this area.

JULIA

MAMA HAS MOVED almost all our things to the
new apartment, but she hasn't touched my room;
I'll be able to stay here as long as possible, and so
can Peter. His bed is still here, and Smuggler's
house, and a few other things.

I haven't been in the new apartment yet; I just
haven't felt like it. Peter and I have walked past
the house. We looked up at our windows on the
second floor, and they looked just like all the
other windows in all the other houses on that
street.

Mama says everything will be all right once we
get used to it.

But I don't want to get used to it!

"You have to," says Mama. "Everyone has to."

I don't feel that way—quite the opposite. You have to put up with all kinds of things, but why should you have to get used to it? When you get used to things, you no longer want to change them. So I'll never get used to it. Never!

It really hit us hard when they didn't pay attention to Peter's last letter either. If I hadn't been so furious I probably would have cried, although I don't any longer. It's much better to be angry than to be sad, because if you're down you just sit around with a long face, but if you're mad you have to *do* something, otherwise you break into splinters.

When I'm angry I'm charged with energy, and Peter too. Now we've told everybody what we planned: that they could have this house to enjoy if it had been up to us. But now that won't happen because the house will be torn down.

I made sure that they understood that it wasn't because I wanted to live in the house, but that I just wanted it to be saved. Almost everybody offered to help. The kids in my class were wonderful. They all agree with me, including Ulla. Sometimes she's O.K.

But I have no intention of moving before the bulldozer comes.

Peter has found out when it's going to be—next Wednesday. We knew it would be soon because lots of stupid, greedy people have been here and written their names on almost everything. They think that they can buy doors and floors and anything they want when the house is destroyed.

But it hasn't been torn down yet!

When it happens, we're going to have a party. We've written a lot of invitations and put them in people's mailboxes, telling them that they can bring their friends—everyone is invited. It's the kind of party where everyone chips in, and we've told them all what to bring.

We're not going to start trouble and throw eggs and tomatoes and things like that at the bulldozer. We just want to show them how much fun they could have here, and give them a chance to be in on it before the house is torn down. The bulldozer too—and if it wants to begin ripping things up in the middle of the party, we won't try to stop it, although it would be very rude, of course. . . .

We have an awful lot to do, because everything has to be ready in time. The place is going to be beautiful! We've cleaned the whole house, and there are going to be flowers and garlands and flags everywhere.

And balloons, naturally.

Lots of people are here helping every day, practically my whole class, and all kinds of people I never even knew before. But now we all know each other.

Tryggve, my teacher, is also here. In the beginning he was running around and talking the way he usually does. He didn't accomplish a single thing, but told everyone what one "really" ought to do, and what fantastic ideas he always came up with in cases like this. He was the bore he usually is. In school you're impressed by things like that, but now, not one bit. No one had time to listen to his talk because everybody had a job to do. Even the girls in my class thought that he ought to be doing something else besides blabbering all the time, and they kept on saying it.

"It's different in school," Birgit said, "but now of all times, when we have work to do!"

We were really pretty sick of it.

"Can't you put a little steam under Tryggve?" I said to Peter.

"I'll try," Peter said. "Do you think he can wash windows?"

The gulls had messed up almost all the windows, and we couldn't have them looking like that during our festivities. So Tryggve had to tackle them. In the beginning he talked more than he worked, but now he has quieted down. Maybe he noticed that you work better that way. He seems quite surprised at his discovery, but the windows are going to be sparkling.

Now I have to start helping again, because we have so much left to do. . . .

JULIA AND PETER

PETER AND I will have to write this together because it's too much for one person to remember. But we won't keep on telling who has written what, because that would be boring. So I'm beginning.

Everything was ready for the party in time—almost. There were more things we wanted to do which we didn't get to, but probably no one noticed because everything else was so lovely, including the weather. The sky was blue.

About half past five in the morning the first people began coming, and after that they just kept coming in streams. Everyone wanted to be there when the bulldozer came.

We thought it would come at seven o'clock, but it didn't, and that gave us time to tell the uninitiated how we were going to greet it, so that the occasion would be as festive as possible.

Shortly after seven some men came to unhinge doors, and take care of all the bits and pieces which had nametags such as Jonsson, Kvist, etc., but they stopped in their tracks when they noticed that they had walked in on the beginning of a party. We offered them coffee, which they accepted, but then they disappeared—we don't know where. Peter thinks they mingled with the guests.

There must have been at least two hundred people here—lots of them children—but there was no danger of overcrowding because the garden is like a park, and they didn't all have to be in the house.

While we were waiting for the bulldozer there were a lot of things to do. You could throw darts, play badminton and croquet and Ping-Pong, the little kids could swing and play in the sand, and there were balls and marbles and jump ropes—all kinds of things. Obviously no one was bored.

When the bulldozer didn't arrive, Julia and I were a bit worried. We were afraid that someone had gone to the authorities and told them about the party, and that at the last minute they had changed their minds and decided not to come today. They could have postponed it to another day when we weren't prepared. What would we do then? We got more worried every minute. It was already half past nine. Time went by too quickly for others, but for us it stood still.

About ten o'clock Nils—the artist—came running. He had been around town trying to find out what was going on. The bulldozer was on the way, he said. It wasn't scheduled to start until ten.

Now it was seven minutes before, and we figured that it would arrive on the dot.

"Anything else?" I asked.

No, everything was as usual in town, Nils told us. The streets were practically empty. I asked him what the guy on the bulldozer was like, and Nils said that he was a heavy, grumpy man, who probably only looked ahead to the usual joyless drudgery the whole day long. Clearly that was all his life consisted of, Nils reflected. But we were going to do our best to cheer him up!

"Maybe he doesn't want to be cheered up," said Tryggve, who was standing nearby.

"We all do," said Nils.

Tryggve didn't seem to agree, but we didn't have time to discuss it because the bulldozer was only a few blocks away. I called out to everybody to get ready. It was five minutes to ten.

Then I caught sight of Elvis Karlsson, who had also received an invitation. I had been on the lookout for him but hadn't spotted him until now. I was afraid that he wouldn't dare show up in this crowd. But there he was, sitting in his spot under Julia's window, where he had hidden something in the ground, and drawn his radiating sun. A small green plant had shot up there, and of course that is what he was watching so carefully.

But I didn't have time to devote to Elvis Karlsson now. Julia and I climbed up on the roof, which we had agreed to do. We perched ourselves on the gable and Smuggler flew up and joined us. Up here he didn't mind participating, but otherwise the festivities didn't seem to amuse him. He was just curious.

We had a marvelous view of the whole garden, and a good piece of the street. The garden was full of people, but the street was empty. There were a lot of games going on under the trees, and everyone had found something fun to do.

Suddenly everything stopped. Everyone was ready. The windows were wide open and there were people at every window, waiting.

"Peter! The bulldozer!" Julia shouted, and pointed to the street. And there it was!

It approached slowly. The street in front of it looked empty and desolate, although it was flooded in sunshine. Julia stared fixedly at the machine and shuddered, and I also had a creepy feeling of gloom and doom.

The gates were wide open to receive the bulldozer. We had also built a large triumphal arch of flowers and leaves and crowned it with letters braided together of pale blue forget-me-nots: WELCOME, it said.

Just as the bulldozer reached the arch, there was a burst of music from under the trees. Tryggve had brought a band along. The only sound was the music. Everything else was quiet.

There was no wind either, whereas before there had been a stiff breeze; we had felt it, sitting up there on the roof. But now the air was still.

The bulldozer stopped. The driver stuck his head out and looked around. Seeing the triumphal arch and hearing the music obviously confused him, and he looked as if he thought he had come to the wrong place.

Then he sat back and continued to push through the gate. He didn't drive carefully. The arch swayed as the bulldozer ripped it along in its wake, and there was a rain of flowers.

This wasn't a good omen. I stood up and signaled that we should let it pass, follow our plans, and let nothing stop us.

There were soap-bubble makers throughout the garden, so that the bulldozer was received by festive music and shimmering bubbles as it proceeded along the path towards the house. Everyone was blowing bubbles; the garden was full; there were people at every window, and Julia and I were up on the roof.

Smuggler didn't blow bubbles, but he was delirious with joy and flew around chasing them, looking just as silly each time he caught them and they burst.

The air glittered. It was a wonderful sight, especially from the roof, but probably also from the ground. For the man sitting in the bulldozer, and not at all prepared for such a reception, it must have been fantastic. The entire bulldozer was surrounded by bubbles, and strewn with forget-me-nots from the triumphal arch.

The man couldn't fail to be moved by it all. But he kept on going.

We waited.

He just kept plowing ahead until he was almost at the door, and then he stopped suddenly. He turned the motor off. Everybody held their breath. The music also stopped.

Julia shot me a questioning look, and I nodded.

She was holding an old brass gramophone horn which sparkled in the sun. She lifted it to her mouth and cried:

"I, the spirit of this house greet you, the spirit of the bulldozer, and welcome you to these festivities which are being held in your honor."

She stopped and sent me a pleading look, but I had a slip on which we had written down the whole speech, so there was nothing to worry about. I fished it out of my pocket and was going to prompt her, when she remembered of her own accord and continued:

"All of us here are very happy to see you because we know that you are the one with power and that you decide the fate of all houses. They can send you wherever they like, but when you stand in front of a house, as you're now doing, it's up to you to decide whether you're going to tear it down—or refuse. You certainly have a great responsibility, and we want you to know we're depending on you. I and everyone else here have

been waiting for you to come and see the house.
We're sure that you'll look at it carefully and
think hard before you go to work on it. We hope

that this beautiful house will be saved, so that
everybody in town will have someplace to meet
and become friends. So it's up to you to decide
our fate today. Therefore, Great Spirit, get out of
your machine and enter my house!"

When Julia had finished her speech, the band
started up anew and soap bubbles again began to
fill the air.

We hurried down from the roof. The driver
was still sitting in the bulldozer. We held our
breath. Would he start the motor again, or would
he come out and look at the house as Julia had
asked him to?

The poor man looked terribly confused sitting
there. By now he probably had a short circuit in
his head. We realized that it wasn't easy for him.
When he still didn't move, we decided to leave
him alone and let him collect himself. The party
was still in full swing.

After a while he looked out—and up towards
the sky, as if he hoped some help would come
from there. The sun was shining right in his face,
he seemed wide awake, and must have been notic-
ing that the sky was blue and that it was an unusually beautiful day.

His eyes were taking in the whole scene.
People, mostly children, were standing around

and looking at him expectantly. They all looked friendly and happy and were nodding to him . . . as if they were waiting. . . .

Gradually it dawned on him that there was a party going on and that he was also invited.

But what about the job he was here to do? He looked at the bulldozer.

The suspense was terrible. Would he start the thing up again? He stared at the levers, grabbed them, kept touching them. But he looked at them in an uninterested way—as if he didn't feel like working. It was obvious that he was going through an inner struggle. He was sighing deeply.

We had agreed not to do anything. Now he had to make up his own mind. We weren't going to try to influence him any more. We had to rely on him!

We saw him hesitate in there, lift his hand, and we thought: Now the game's up. Now he's going to start! But he didn't. Instead he opened the door—and left the bulldozer!

A small child was already there with a glass of raspberry juice, and another came with a piece of cake. He accepted both as if he were in a haze, and began munching away with an absentminded look. Elvis Karlsson appeared with a straw, which he accepted.

"This is the way to do it," said a very little child, and blew into his straw so that the juice in the tumbler bubbled. The bulldozerman did the same and seemed to be enjoying himself.

I really think he felt welcome.

But then something happened.

Two men came marching up the path. We knew them, but I mustn't tell their names, because one has to be tactful, Peter says. But I can say that they had something to do with tearing down the house—had everything to do with it. They approached with big steps, looking very bossy, slapping each other in the back and acting very friendly.

But the closer they came to the house the more angry they looked, and when they caught sight of the bulldozerman they looked absolutely menacing. There he was standing in the sunshine surrounded by a lot of children. He was really the reason for the party, so everyone was watching him while he was bubbling away with his straw, and we were feeding him cake because he seemed hungry.

The men elbowed their way up and began shouting at him. He didn't say anything; he looked surprised, as if he hardly heard what they said, and continued to drink his raspberry juice and eat cake. That left the two men to argue with each other instead, but we couldn't hear what they were saying because of the music and the talk all around. We could tell that they were angry though—their faces were red and they kept on gesticulating with their arms. They didn't try to act friendly any longer.

We tried to offer them some juice and cake, because it was meant for everyone, but one of them shooed us away as if we were flies, and the other one took the juice but not the cake, but spilled it all because he was so jittery. We refilled his cup, and then he did accept the cake, which made the first guy even madder, so that he took both cake and juice from the other man and threw them away. What a way to act!

Everybody was kind of shaken up, but we didn't show it because we had decided that no matter what they did, we would be courteous, so that they wouldn't have any complaints against us.

That was the hardest part!

Then one of the guys glared at me and asked where there was a telephone (he was the one who threw away the juice and the cake). He just had to get to a telephone that minute, he yelled.

I told him I would show him the way, and

walked ahead of him into the house. I swear I didn't plan this in advance, but I executed my masterstroke!

Somehow I didn't take him to the room where the telephone was.

"Please, this way," I said, but then I went in the wrong direction.

He didn't suspect anything, because there is a small vestibule which leads to the door. Then there is another door, and behind it a bathroom. I showed him in there, and naturally he thought he would find the telephone. When he walked in I shut the door and bolted it! The name Strand was on the bolt, because almost everything in the house was tagged.

I got myself out of there fast. But when I got into the hall, I could hear that the old man had discovered that he was in the wrong place. The other one had probably taken off, because his car wasn't there.

I didn't tell Peter what I had done. I didn't tell anyone; I just didn't want to talk about it.

After a while I heard some shouting which seemed strange, because everyone was having such a good time, so I went to see what was up.

What a miserable sight I saw!

The bathroom window is quite hard to open because the frame is warped, but the man had gotten it open and made a desperate try to get out, but had gotten himself stuck. There he sat like a stopper, his cheeks looked like apples, his arms were swinging around like windmills, and he was swearing so that you could almost see the smoke rise.

"What's the matter with that man?" said a little boy who climbed up and placed a funny hat on the man's head. Since everyone was supposed to be happy at the party, others came and tried to cheer the old man up with streamers and balloons, but it didn't work. He was just a hopeless, grouchy old man!

I got help to get him out of there, and it was just as well because he was so nasty.

The man in the bulldozer had a much nicer disposition, although you wouldn't have thought so from the beginning. He was obviously enjoying the party, because when Elvis and Nils started to paint the bulldozer, he helped them. It looked fantastic—like a big beautiful toad, or grasshopper, or something like that.

Then he sat down in the bulldozer and drove it around for the fun of it. He made it act like an animal; the kids could feed it, and I did, too.

Yes, the party was a great success, and the time went by too quickly.

Peter and I had decided that we would disappear when the party was at its peak. Everyone seemed happy, so there was nothing left for us to do. At that point Peter came and whispered to me:

"Let's sneak away, Julia! We've done our share!"

When nobody was watching, we slipped out through a back door, leaving the others behind, and for a long time we heard the sound of laughter behind us.

"Do you think they'll leave the house standing now?" I asked.

But Peter didn't have any answer to that.

"There's no way of knowing yet," he said. "They can come back another day."

"I don't think they'll dare," I said.

Peter didn't agree. "They could bring the police along," he said.

"But I don't think that the police would want to go against everyone's wishes. They'll have to decide when and if they'll come, just like the bulldozer."

"Don't know," said Peter. "But no matter what happens, we've been able to demonstrate how

176

everyone feels about it. If they still tear down the house at least they'll know that they're doing something wrong."

"I don't believe they'd ever do it," I said.

"Let's hope you're right," said Peter.

I wanted him to believe as I did, he *had* to, because that would make it even more certain. But he just shook his head and said that he couldn't be sure of anything, but that even if we failed this time, maybe we would succeed the next, or the next. . . .

"We're going to win this time," I said, because I believe it.

Peter nodded. "But you know you won't live in this house any longer, Julia. You realize that, don't you?"

Yes, I do understand that, even though I don't think about it. All I want is for the house to be saved . . . !

How I wish I could promise that the house will be saved. But how can I? All we can do is hope, Julia.

At least we know that we have everybody on our side, and that helps. We didn't talk any more about it.

We walked through the modern section where Julia and her mother were going to live, and ran into some kids playing. They had built a city in the sand.

Suddenly, a kid with a bulldozer made like the real thing came along and set it down right in the middle of their city. While the other kids stood by and looked on, he demolished one house after another with his bulldozer. He was obviously enjoying himself—he didn't look very nice. All at once the other kids began to cry.

Julia looked terrified.

"They should have been at the party," she said. "I forgot to invite them. . . ."

"One always forgets someone," was all I could say.

Things are always more complicated than they seem. We got away from there as fast as we could.

First we stopped at my place to see if Smuggler was there. He had soon gotten tired of the party and left. I had suspected as much, and had left the window open so that he could get in if he wanted to.

We whistled to him from the outside. I have a special whistle which means that we're going on an outing, and that he can join us if he wants to. He was home and came flying out like a flash.

"Are you coming along?" I asked him.

Yes, he was. But he flies in all directions, and

sometimes keeps quite far away from us. The main thing is that he's happy. He is very careful about keeping in touch with us the whole time. We hear his hooting here and there, and he never loses sight of us. Then all of a sudden he'll come zooming down and settle on my shoulder.

After parties I always have a longing for the sea, and so does Julia, so that's where we went. Waves are so soothing. The air was like crystal, and it was at its best over the sea, unobstructed by trees and houses.

"Only by boats and birds," Julia mused.

"That's right. Only by boats and birds. . . ."

We were standing on a cliff with the woods behind us, facing the sea. There was a brisk breeze. But suddenly all was still. And then we saw a strange sight.

Out in the water, swaying a bit above the waves, white horses were grazing in a field. We saw them distinctly—one of them even galloping. Then a red ball came rolling along the field and stopped, while the other horses went galloping off in different directions. But they gathered again and continued to graze as before. The red ball was still lying there.

And a ship with white sails was slowly gliding over the waves, right under the meadow where the horses were grazing. The mast brushed right under their hoofs.

Julia held my hand tight. Her eyes were bright. "Are we seeing ghosts?" she whispered.

"No, it's a mirage," I told her.

We watched the scene until it vanished. Neither of us had seen a mirage before, and for a long time we couldn't say a word.

But then we heard Smuggler hooting from the woods behind us, and that brought us back to reality.

We scrambled down to the beach. A strong wind had blown up again. But the air was warm, so we took our shoes off and ran barefoot in the sand.

Then I felt that I must be the happiest person in the world, and so did Peter. We have seen a mirage!

A mirage! It was as if we had given it to each other as a present. We both said thank you to each other at the same moment because we were so happy.

Then we ran along the shore, splashing in the waves. Sometimes Peter was ahead, and sometimes I was.

At one point Peter stopped and looked at the sand.

Someone had written the name ELVIS there.

"Elvis . . ." Peter exclaimed.

He was probably thinking of Elvis Karlsson, the little kid, but I don't think it was that Elvis, although I had no way of knowing.

He told me that he's going to give me a sunflower.

Anyway, it's much better to write your name in the sand than on doors and floors and all over the place, the way they did in our house. Peter thought so too, and we laughed.

But I felt sorry for "them" too, because they had never seen a mirage. Everyone should see one, and then they could never again be greedy, grabbing everything in sight, and things like that.

We kept on running; we never got tired, and all over the beach we wrote PETER . . . SMUGGLER . . . JULIA . . . SMUGGLER . . . JULIA . . . PETER . . .

But the wind was behind us, and together with the waves it swept away the names, so that we had to keep on writing over and over again:

SMUGGLER . . . PETER . . . JULIA . . . SMUGGLER . . . JULIA . . . PETER . . .

MARIA GRIPE

recently won the highest international award in children's literature, the Hans Christian Andersen Medal. This award was given in recognition of the universal appeal of her books, which have now been translated into thirteen languages. Her much-loved HUGO AND JOSEPHINE trilogy won her both the Astrid Lindgren Prize and the Nils Holgersson Plaque, the most important Scandinavian prize for children's books, and was also made into a film.

Maria Gripe is now engaged in adapting some of her stories for Swedish television. She lives in Sweden, with her husband Harald Gripe, an artist who has illustrated most of her books, and her daughter, also a writer.